TAKEDOWN

GRAHAM MARKS

Catnip

Also by Graham Marks
Faultline

CATNIP BOOKS
Published by Catnip Publishing Ltd.
Islington Business Centre
3-5 Islington High Street
London N1 9LQ

This edition published 2007
1 3 5 7 9 10 8 6 4 2

A CIP catalogue record for this book is available from the British Library

ISBN 13: 978-1-84647-022-9

Printed in Poland

www.catnippublishing.co.uk

1

2667. It had been the strangest year, and so far it was only three months old. Weather patterns, never the easiest things to predict, had gone mad; the annual polar storms hadn't materialized in the Northern Hemisphere and ravenous wolf packs had moved south out of the Saharan taiga forests, creating havoc; Australia was in the grip of a monsoon season the like of which had never been seen and the Japanese ice cap had begun to melt – with disastrous consequences to the Stilt Cities.

As if that weren't enough, the San Andreas coastline (all that was left of the west coast of America after the Great Quake in 2110 had finally done what it'd been threatening to do for centuries) had gone critical again when a string of dormant volcanoes unexpectedly erupted.

Spenzer Timor was at his workstation, scanning the dozens of hypertext screens that surrounded him, trying to make some kind of sense of the flood of information cascading in front of his eyes. It was his job, as head of Central Data Control, to keep the President up to speed on what was going on in the world outside the United Southern States.

He worked on the top floor of the 50-storey Integrated™ Building in downtown Johannesburg, the USS capital, and sometimes felt as if he was actually a physical part of its complex computer network and not the man supposed to be in charge of it. Sometimes days went by when he didn't see a real human being, just faintly ghostlike holocasts of people virting in and out of his space.

You didn't really have meetings any more, VirtualContact had made them unnecessary, but sometimes Spenzer missed the real thing – the smell of another person, the tiny details of weight and size that a virt session never gave you.

He was deep in thought, puzzling over the latest data-set – evidence of a curious shift in the earth's magnetic field – when the red light flashed on. For a moment he thought he'd imagined it, that he'd blink and it wouldn't be there any more, but it was. Then a holocast of the President's Secretary-General, Garston Pyce, flicked on.

"Timor," he said. "We need an eftee-eff, as of now!"

Pyce was well known for his use of street slang, he thought it made him appear a man of the people and it took Spenzer a moment to click that he was being asked – ordered, really – to come to the Palace for an urgent face-to-face meeting.

"I'll call a shuttle, sir," he replied.

"There's one waiting for you at the flight deck on your floor," said Pyce, his holocast disappearing without another word.

Spenzer sat back in his chair, pulling at his lower lip. What was going on? Why the sudden urgency – why the need to actually see the President? Frowning to himself he logged in with his staff, telling them he'd be away for at least a couple of hours, and left for the flight deck.

It was midday, and even though he probably wouldn't

have to walk in the open he put on his UV-mesh gloves and white solar helmet, flipping its tinted eye shades down. Better safe than sorry, as even black skin was no protection against the rad levels at noon, and Spenzer had no wish to go blind in his mid-twenties.

A Palace shuttle was hovering by the deck exit as he walked through the doors, its charm-drive motors burbling quietly to themselves. It was pre-programmed, so all he had to do was get in and sit down.

Johannesburg seemed to go on for miles. It had long ago swallowed up Pretoria, but the old capital, now merely one of many districts, was where the Presidential Palace was still located. It was madly inconvenient, but historical reasons were always given for not moving the ceremonial home closer to the central tech-hub.

The shuttle's heavily tinted window allowed Spenzer a magnificent view of the capital. From this vast megasprawl – the word "city" couldn't describe it any more – came the rule of law that governed everyone and everything south of the 20th Parallel. And for the first time in his life, he was about to meet the man at the very top of the power pyramid.

Spenzer Timor couldn't say he was really looking forward to the experience. Something, somewhere, had gone wrong and he had a nasty feeling in the pit of his stomach that he was going to get the blame.

2

Spenzer was led into a relatively small, beautifully furnished room with a long wooden table running down the centre of it. Ten other people were there, most of whom he recognized and a couple that he'd actually met in person. The President hadn't yet arrived, and there was no sign of Garston Pyce either.

A woman stood up and walked towards him. "You must be Timor from Central Data," she said, holding out her hand.

"Yes," said Spenzer, nodding as he shook it.

"I'm Cardoza from Scientific, out in Maraisburg," she went on. "Any idea what this is all about?"

"None at all. I was told to come here by Pyce."

"I think *asked* is a better way of describing it, Timor."

Spenzer swung round to see Garston Pyce walking into the room. Before he had a chance to say anything else the Secretary-General strode past him and went to the head of the table. "The President has asked me to brief you before he arrives, so, if you'll all sit down, I'll get started."

Pyce began speaking in that annoying way most politicians have of treating their audience as if they were very young children. "You will, of course, all know the name Simon Tellkind," he said, pausing. "The man who discovered the Charm Principle some six hundred years ago . . ."

"Six hundred and sixty, to be precise," said an older man opposite Spenzer, the head of Psychic Research – if he remembered correctly.

"Thank you, Parmar." The Secretary-General made his mouth smile. "To continue . . . It cannot have escaped the notice of all present here that there have been some exceedingly odd things happening on a global, as well as a local level – I need not go into detail now. Suffice to say, every one of the Nation States has been monitoring these, shall we say, *bizarre*, occurrences.

"We received a coded hot-link call from the Pan-American Union capital in Buenos Aires late last night, President-to-President." Pyce waited for a moment, as if to let this fact sink in. "It was alarming, to say the least, and we need your joint input before we can reply."

"Cut the speech-making, Garston," said a woman whom Spenzer knew to be the head of Inter-Planetary Activity. "Tell us why we're here."

"I was just coming to that." Pyce looked annoyed, but carried on. "PAU scientists up in the Dallas Cold Zone, researching sub-zero molecular grafting, have apparently discovered some disturbing facts – the reason, so they say, for what's going on. They've called it the Scattering Effect."

"Called what the Scattering Effect?" said Parmar in a gruff, annoyed voice.

"They say that their research shows there's a hidden by-product – one of them referred to it as a 'subatomic exhaust' – from charm-drive engines," continued Pyce, while behind him the wall restructured itself into a number of screens covered with complex formulae. "It's so small it can hardly be measured, in fact no one has until now . . . no one's bothered to look because they didn't know it was there."

"And what does this so-called subatomic exhaust do, Garston?" asked Parmar.

"To put it crudely," the Secretary-General glared at the head of Psychic Research, "it randomly unglues atomic structures, and has been doing so – as you so kindly pointed out a moment ago – for six hundred and sixty years. The universe is literally falling apart."

"Impossible!" snorted Vena Cardoza. "The Science Agency would have noticed before!"

"We're noticing it now," said Pyce, pointing at Spenzer. "Ask him. Timor, you've got the most up-to-date information: is there *anywhere* on the planet that's not got problems?"

"It's worldwide, Secretary-General, and we've also had some very strange data from out-of-system satellites, as I-PA can verify." The woman from Inter-Planetary Activity nodded in agreement.

"The Dallas experiments have apparently been duplicated at the Arecibo laboratory," Pyce went on, picking up the file. "The Pan Americans only released the information when they were sure it was accurate."

"Is the situation reversible?" asked Cardoza. "Can we halt this . . . this Scattering Effect?"

"As far as I know, the answer to both those questions is no," said Pyce. "But that's why you are all here today – the President wants to hear what you have to say about the matter; he wants to know what you think can be done."

"And just how long do we have to save the world?" said Parmar, sarcastically.

"The President will be here in an hour," replied Pyce, ignoring Parmar's comment and getting up. "Do what you can."

There was a moment's stunned silence as they all watched Pyce leave the room, and then all hell broke out. Arms waved, voices were raised and tempers flared – if Garston Pyce had tripped the counter on a null-bomb, dropped it on the table and walked out, the reaction to what he'd done wouldn't have been any different.

Spenzer felt numbed. He couldn't quite take in what the Secretary-General had said – partly because he'd said it in such a matter-of-fact way, but mostly because the idea of the universe falling apart was a concept that had the effect of seizing up your ability to think straight. If at all. Looking round the room he could see everyone else was feeling much the same way.

3

Vena Cardoza was the first person to get a grip on herself. Standing up she moved round to the head of the table, where Pyce had left the file. Opening it, she scanned the first few pages of megafiche, tapping a couple of information matrixes to activate them. She read some of the scrolling text, switched the page off and then rapped the table with her knuckles.

"We have fifty-five minutes to come up with something sensible to say to the President," she said as people turned to look at her. "I suggest we start by looking at the file the Secretary-General has left behind – I, for one, want to check those figures."

"You can check all you want, Vena," said a grey-haired man, his white face so lined it looked like it'd been drawn on. "I know both those research teams – Dallas and Arecibo – and they're the best there is. Let's not waste any time checking facts when what we need is ideas."

The room had calmed down now, the tension bubble had burst and people were focusing back on the problem in hand.

"How can something that's been around for so long have such an appalling side-effect, and no one noticed?" said Spenzer. "It's like suddenly finding the *wheel* causes cancer!"

"The wheel's just an object," said the old man. "It

can be fatal if you put one at each corner of a box and hurtle down a steep hill with no brakes. We've known for centuries that for every action there's a *re*action, we just assumed that, with Tellkind's Charm Principle mankind had found the answer to all its prayers – an incredibly cheap, totally clean and completely unlimited source of power."

"And nothing's ever that easy, Barron?" said Vena.

"Precisely," said the old man. "And for over half a millennium we've cheerfully ignored the fact. We did it with fossil fuel, we did it again with nuclear power – why change the habits of so many lifetimes?"

"That's the problem, isn't it?" sighed Spenzer. "We can't change anything in the past – once Pythagoras had conceived his Theorem, and Einstein his Theory, they were there. They couldn't be *un*thought."

"They could have been changed," said Vena as she pored over the file. She was now looking at some encapsulated vid-clips running on the page she'd turned to. "If they didn't work properly."

"$E = MC^2$ works fine," said Spenzer. "It's just a very *dangerous* idea, and nothing can change that."

"Unless . . ." Barron stood up and went to look out of the window.

"Unless what?" Vena glanced across the room, frowning.

"Unless the thought never happened, or it wasn't completed," said Barron. "The eighteenth-century poet Coleridge never finished 'Kubla Khan', one of his most famous poems, because someone interrupted his train of thought – the ending was lost for ever, all because of a knock at his front door."

"Unfortunately we can't knock on Simon Tellkind's door, can we, Barron?" said Vena, going back to the file. "And even if we could, and we made him forget the Charm Principle, think what catastrophic damage *that* would do to our time-line – everything would change!"

By now everyone in the room had stopped what they were doing and was listening to this conversation. Questions started to fly back and forth, but Spenzer noticed that the old man, Barron, wasn't paying much attention. In fact he'd gone over to a meta-comp screen and was playing with what looked like an extraordinarily complex algebraic maths problem. He went over to talk to him.

"I don't think we've ever met," he said, "not even in virt – I'm Spenzer Timor, head of Central Data."

"Nice to meet you," said the old man, eyes still glued to the screen. "I'm Stave Barron, from Tech-Genesis."

"The research and development outfit in Cape Town?" Spenzer looked surprised. "How did you get here so quickly?"

"I was up, visiting Ms Cardoza," explained Barron, making a note on one of the many sub-screens. "Pure luck I was here, really."

"What are you doing?"

"Checking Tellkind's formulae."

"For what?"

"Mistakes, anomalies and – the more I look at it – possible areas for improvement," said Barron, standing back and scrutinizing his work. To Spenzer it looked like nothing more than a senseless jumble of letters, numbers and symbols, but his speciality was information: mathematics was an unintelligible foreign language to him.

"There's a phrase I've heard used in old vids," Barron went on. "How did it go? Something like 'If it isn't broken, leave it alone'?"

"It's 'If it ain't broke, don't fix it'," said Spenzer, whose hobby was collecting pre-millennium vids.

"Right," smiled Barron, "and I think that's the attitude everyone's had towards Tellkind's work . . . this may be the first time *any*one's really scrutinized it. Mr Timor, I wonder if you'd mind . . ."

"Of course," said Spenzer. "Carry on."

Spenzer left the old man to his work and went back to the table to join Vena Cardoza as she flicked through the megafiche pages, the thin, circuit-coated paper seeming almost alive with information. And very depressing reading it made, especially as there was less than an hour in which to come up with some kind of solution to the cataclysmic problem they all now faced.

A quarter of an hour later, as he stood with a small knot of people discussing the possibility of devising exhaust traps or maybe subatomic filters, Spenzer saw Stave Barron wave a hand at Vena Cardoza, asking her to come and look at something on the screens.

Vena detached herself from the group she was at the centre of and came to join the old man. "What's up?" she said.

11

"Tell me what you think." Barron pointed at one particular area on the main screen. "I'd say *that's* where the problem is, but you'd only know it well after the event. Tellkind would have had no reason to suspect, none at all."

Others in the room had begun to gather round the meta-comp screen, a low murmur filling the room.

"And if you make this *small* change," Barron inserted a slug of data from one of the sub-screens on top of a dense jumble of calculations – "you harmlessly vent what the Dallas boys called subatomic exhaust, yet the Charm Principle still works perfectly."

"Amazing!" Vena shook her head in admiration. "A stunning piece of lateral thought, Stave . . . but how can it help us now? I mean, this innovation of yours is just a tad too late to be of any use. Six hundred and seventy years too late."

"But at least we know *why* it's happening," said Spenzer excitedly, "and now we can stop the process carrying on as well!"

"I'm not trying to undermine what Stave has done," said Vena, raising her hands to calm the rising babble of animated chatter in the room. "It's a quite spectacular mental leap, but it's *not* a solution. And we're running out of time . . ."

She looked around the room at the faces staring back at her, the hope Barron's discovery had given people fading fast as they all realized she was right – knowing what was wrong, and how to put it right, wasn't going to help them now.

"Ordinarily I'd say you were correct," smiled Barron, seemingly unperturbed by Vena's comments. "But I do believe Mr Parmar might have some useful input here. Josh? Could you tell them about the TRiP project?"

The head of Psychic Research reddened slightly as everyone turned to look at him. "Now, Stave?" he said. "Are you *sure*?"

"As good a stage in the proceedings as any, Josh."

"Right . . ." said Parmar, nervously. "I'll try and explain this as simply as possible. TRiP, or Temporal Ribbon Placement, is a process which allows us to remove the electrical essence of a living thing – its soul, if you will – and transmit it along the time-line and into a host mind.

"Our experiments have shown that the host mind is completely taken over by the TRiP subject," Parmar continued, "but the process has only been done successfully – and over *very* short distances, maximum a couple of days – with lower life forms . . . mice, cats, etc. We do, though, *appear* to have made a phenomenal breakthrough."

"For those of you who haven't quite grasped the full import of what Josh is saying," said Barron, looking round the room, "what Temporal Ribbon Placement boils down to is – time travel. Only backwards and, so far, only in tiny jumps, but time travel nonetheless. As he so rightly says, a phenomenal breakthrough . . ."

"You've sent a *cat* back in time?" said Vena.

"We've sent the binary electrical *essence* of a cat back," replied Parmar. "Put it into a mouse, actually!"

4

Josh Parmar – Professor Parmar, to give him his full title – looked like he wanted to find a convenient hole in Time to disappear into. He was unused to being the centre of attention and was discovering very quickly and that he didn't like it at all. The questions were flying at him, nineteen to the dozen, and everyone was talking at once.

"How opportune," said Vena Cardoza, as she once again took command of the increasingly fractious and unruly gathering. "Just when we need it someone's invented time travel. What a coincidence, I don't think . . . How long have you had this thing under wraps, Parmar?"

"It's been a classified project, President's Eyes Only."

"How long?"

"A year, maybe fourteen months," admitted Parmar.

"Incredible! You find what amounts to a scientific Holy Grail and keep it a secret for over a year? But . . ." Vena stopped and shot a frowning glance at Barron. "Wait a minute . . . so how did you know about it, Stave?"

"The idea came from us in the first place," the old man replied, smiling broadly. "That's what Tech-Genesis is all about – having ideas. Once we've had them we pass them on to the relevant Directorate to see if they can actually do anything with them, whether they'll work in the real world. Put this down to synchronicity, Vena."

"The right idea at the right time?"

"It happens," said Barron. "In fact, *as* it happens, this project was about to get closed down."

"Why?" asked Spenzer, who'd been watching events unfold with fascination.

"Because it worked too well." Barron turned to look at him. Seeing his puzzled expression he went on: "Time travel is probably the most dangerous thing ever invented. In the wrong hands, as you yourself said, Vena, the results could be catastrophic."

"You must've known this from the outset," said Vena, "so why go ahead?"

"You're a scientist, Vena," smile Barron, his lined face creasing like old leather. "You know we're in love with concepts, not consequences. It was pure research until Parmar and his team proved they could do it."

"So if this hadn't happened," Vena indicated the meeting in general, "the project would have just disappeared, like it'd never existed?"

"That's a very naïve comment, Vena," tutted Barron. "History is littered with ideas that were too dangerous for their time, as you well know – Copernicus, Galileo . . ."

"But their ideas surfaced *eventually*, Stave," said Vena, "so you couldn't have hidden the TRiP project for ever."

"Maybe not," nodded Barron, "but believe me, we were going to try."

"You're taking this whole affair in an incredibly calm fashion, Stave," said Vena. "We're told the world is falling apart and you coolly figure out why, not to mention how to fix it, and then you cap it all by announcing the invention of time travel!"

"I've never been one for getting over-excited; experience has taught me it tends to muddy the waters," said Barron. "And anyway, I'm a pragmatist at heart – think, then panic, has always been my motto."

"I hate to break up this fascinating philosophical discussion," said Spenzer, looking at his watch, "but the President will be here in ten minutes – is time travel the solution we're going to tell him we've come up with?"

"Unless anyone has some other bright ideas?" Barron glanced round the room; no one, it appeared, did. "Then I'd say we don't have any choice *but* to suggest it."

"We haven't yet tried to send a *lower* primate back, Barron," Parmar shook his head. "We've no idea what will happen to a human being – don't even know if it'll work!"

"Looks like now's the time you're going to have to find out," said Barron.

Spenzer Timor had thought his involvement with the project, code named Take-Over, would end with the close of the presidential briefing. He wasn't a scientist, and he knew nothing about the technical aspects of anything, so he assumed he'd be out of the loop from now on. Of no further use.

At 7.30 the next morning, as he came out of the lift, he'd thought it odd that the polarized glass walls of his cubicle were completely darkened – didn't remember leaving them that way the night before – and was taken aback to be stopped from using his voice key to get in by someone he'd never seen before.

"ID," said the man, holding out a small sensor pad.

"What?" Spenzer was confused. He hadn't seen the man sitting at a nearby desk and couldn't work out what was going on.

"Security check, sir," he said. "Just a formality."

"To get into my own office?"

"You have a visitor, sir."

Now even more confused, Spenzer forgot what to do for a moment; he saw the security guard point at the sensor and then he placed his thumb on the pad, watching an indicator light go green. "May I go in now?" he asked. The man nodded and Spenzer told the door to unlock and pushed it open, wondering as he did so how his visitor had managed to override his personal security.

Secretary-General Pyce was sitting in his chair, which explained everything. There was nowhere he didn't have access to.

"Knowing you are an early starter," said Pyce, "I decided to get this meeting out of the way before any of your staff arrived."

Spenzer glanced at his virt console and Pyce caught the look.

"I prefer an eftee-eff in this case, Timor." Pyce waved at Spenzer's other chair. "Sit down."

Spenzer was now an integral part of Project Take-Over. His deputy had been put in temporary charge of Central Data Control and he'd left his 50th-floor office not knowing when he'd return.

Along with Vena Cardoza, Stave Barron and Josh

Parmar's team, he was now working out of a nondescript building somewhere in the Pretoria sprawl. Working *and* living. Security was so tight you could hardly breathe.

Spenzer's first job was to find the man they would send back in time – or, more accurately, the man whose "electrical essence", to quote Parmar, would be transmitted back down the time-line to completely take over the mind of some unsuspecting member of the general public. His second job was to find the right unsuspecting member of the general public.

He began by scouring the information meta-banks – vast organic computers that detailed every living person in the continental USS – for possible candidates to go on this bizarre and dangerous mission. While he did that, the others started brainstorming the real problem. Finding out if doing it was actually possible.

It took Spenzer 72 hours, almost non-stop, to come up with a short list. Once he'd devised the dossier of special qualities each person had to be matched against – intelligence, psychological profile, personal background, professional record, security rating, etc., etc. – he wrote a match-and-compare program. Name after name was run through the algorithm at a blinding speed until, finally, he had a file of seven people who fitted the bill.

Reading it as he went to give the document to Pyce, there was one person who seemed to him to be perfect. Line Sgt Dachron Amok, 2445619/T. Single, 25 years old, no living relatives; First Class degree in Tech Engineering, with honours; trained in unarmed combat, anti-terrorist tactics and guerrilla warfare. Also described as mildly psychopathic. You would, thought Spenzer as he knocked on Pyce's door, need to be a bit mad to go on a mission like this.

Dachron Amok had no idea why he was sitting in this characterless room in some stupid building in the boondocks of Pretoria. He'd been summarily hauled off the search-and-destroy mission up north and flown straight back to the capital. No reasons given, but then he was a soldier first and a person second – as he was always being reminded. It was what he disliked most about his job.

As he paced the room, not even bothering to look out of the window (there was absolutely *nothing* to see, so why waste the time?) he constantly snapped his fingers. *KLIK-KLIK-KLIKETY-KLIK.* It was like a mantra: it calmed him down and kept his thoughts from racing away, becoming confused and making him angry. *KLIK-KLIK-KLIKETY-KLIK.*

Dachron Amok didn't like losing his temper, unless he positively had to – to get his own way. Flying off the handle was always his last option, but if someone didn't come and get him and tell him what the *hell* was going on he was going to have to use it pretty soon. *KLIK-KLIK-KLIKETY-KLIK...*

"He's the best?" said Garston Pyce as he watched a screen showing Dachron Amok prowling about the room like a caged animal.

"According to the Psych people," said Spenzer. "He's the

only one who doesn't really seem to care what happens to him; got no real sense of fear."

"Have the others seen him?"

"Not yet," said Spenzer. "I wanted your approval before I told them we had a pilot."

"Pilot?"

"That's what they're calling the person who'll go back."

"How soon?" asked Pyce.

"As soon as I find the recipient – the host he'll take over," replied Spenzer wearily. "If you OK him I can start on that right away."

"Tell them we've found their man," said Pyce. "He will agree to go, won't he?"

"Apparently he's the type that relishes a challenge."

"Well, he's certainly got one on *this* mission." Pyce switched off the screen and walked to the door. "Don't let me keep you from your work, Timor."

The USS databanks, huge though they were, didn't hold the kind of information Spenzer needed for the next part of his job. Simon Tellkind, the scientist who devised the Charm Principle, did so sometime in the year 2007 – according to the history books. He needed to find out about someone who lived over 600 years ago in England.

And to all intents and purposes England didn't exist any more as a power-base. All records had been moved to Madrid in 2450 and the island abandoned by the two per cent of the population that actually owned and governed it. Spenzer contacted the European State Records

Department, UK Division, and requested a complete download on Tellkind.

When it arrived he found there was precious little in the file about the man who had given the world such an amazing discovery as the Charm Principle. Born in 1960, he'd had an ordinary enough life – for a genius. Educated at Oxford and in America, he seemed to have been a very lonely person, completely dedicated to his work. Everything seemed quite ordinary until the year his incredible invention was announced, when Tellkind just disappeared from view.

There were no signs of any public engagements; no tax, social security or health records, in fact nothing to show that he hadn't died. In a world, even then, when governments were almost more obsessive than they were now about keeping tabs on people, one very important man's slate appeared to have been wiped clean from the age of 47 until an official death announcement in 2045.

Spenzer began taking his professional life apart, bit by bit, examining every part of it. The more he looked the more he was sure that what he was reading was a carefully edited rewrite. Spenzer remembered a book he'd scanned once – George Orwell's *1984* – where history was constantly revised and amended to make it the way it *should* be, not the way it actually *was*.

Why they'd found it necessary to do the same kind of thing to Tellkind he had no idea, but it was obvious that someone somewhere had wanted the man to become invisible. Which made his job even more difficult.

His initial idea had been to locate a co-worker or close

associate and use him as the target for Amok, but he could find no names: there was no information on who Tellkind had worked with, or where. Spenzer had hit a spectacular dead-end.

Sitting in front of his screens he idly scrolled through the decade before Tellkind "vanished", eyes flicking over the information as his mind tried to figure out what to do next. He was just about to go and have a word with Stave Barron when a date caught his attention: 31 January 1990. Tellkind had become the godfather to the son of someone called Richard Anthony.

Spenzer stopped the scrolling and brought up the detail. Amongst all the dry academic and professional information it was the one piece of social interaction he'd seen. Just out of interest he grabbed the name "Richard Anthony" and saved it to a new file. This man had to be someone special, someone who could be of use to them, and he needed to find out more about him . . . and the only place to do that was in America.

Deep inside the Wasatch Mountains in Utah, under 200 metres of solid rock, the Mormon Church still operated its huge microfilm and computer-based Granite Mountain Records Vault. This was an archive of everyone who had ever lived. Well, almost everyone; since 1938, when the Church began to systematically collect records, researchers had scoured the world for information to add to their database and they now had the details of billions of people stored. Finding out about someone who lived in the last half of the twentieth century shouldn't be such a problem.

5

"It's a suicide mission, then," said Dachron. He was in another room now, surrounded by a group of people whose names he'd forgotten the moment he'd been introduced to them. One of them, the woman, had just finished telling him what they wanted him to do.

"No," said Vena Cardoza, "we can pretty much guarantee you won't die in transit. If everything goes according to plan you will, however, have complete control of a body – you will *become* another person in 2007. This way we won't have introduced an 'extra' person into a time-line it doesn't belong to."

"Terrific," Dachron nodded to himself. "But there's no way back, is there? It's first class travel on a one-way ticket."

"You *could* put it like that," said Vena, looking at her colleagues for support.

"Can't think of any *other* way to put it."

"You're right, Line Sgt Amok." Stave Barron got up, smiling. "In a way it *is* a suicide mission . . . If you go you will cease to exist in the here and now. But if it works, as we think it will, you *will* exist in another time frame."

"In someone else's body."

"Yes."

"Weird."

"Yes again," agreed Stave.

23

"Why me?" asked Dachron

"You came out as the best person we could find for the job," said Vena.

"You guys think I'm crazy, don't you?" Dachron looked at each person in the room; only the old man didn't look away, embarrassed.

"You do seem to have a – how shall I say? – a *different* way of approaching things, Dachron." Stave spread his hands out to include everyone. "We need someone to change history, and an *ordinary* person just won't do."

"Flattery isn't something I'm used to in my job," said Dachron. "But I suppose it's all you've got, since you can't offer me money to take this assignment . . . Run me through it one more time, so I've got a complete handle on the whole thing."

Stave cracked his knuckles, straightened his jacket and began to talk. He explained once more about the newly-discovered problem with Simon Tellkind's Charm Principle, the one that meant that the world was literally coming unstuck as he spoke. He went on to tell Dachron that a relatively simple change to a seemingly insignificant part of the equation would get rid of the problem, yet still mean the Principle worked.

"If someone went back, found Tellkind and explained to him about this small alteration *before* his work was completed and published, there would be no error," said Stave. "Taking this to its logical conclusion, therefore, you can see that no error means no subatomic exhaust and hence no Scattering Effect. Problem solved in one fell swoop!"

"Very neat, but what about me?" queried Dachron.

"You'd be an ex-policeman called Richard Anthony, aged forty-seven, married, with two children – and you'd own a business called MetroPol Ltd, some sort of private investigation company," said Spenzer, referring to the megafiche file in his hand. "Sounds just up your street."

"Convenient, him being an ex-cop and all – but forty-seven? That's twice as old as I am now!" frowned Dachron. "Haven't you got someone a bit younger?"

"We thought you'd be happy it's a man," said Vena.

"You'd've tried to put me in a *woman*'s body?"

"Bad joke, I apologize," said Vena. "No, of course we wouldn't—"

"So, Dachron," Stave butted in, "will you go?"

"What haven't you told me?"

"Sorry?"

"There's always something they don't tell you on the *really* dangerous stuff," said Dachron. "At least, not until it's too late to stop or do anything about it."

"I suppose the deadline would come under that heading." Stave cracked his knuckles again.

"What deadline?"

"Should everything go according to plan you'll only have seven days in which to find Simon Tellkind."

"I knew it. How come?" enquired Dachron.

"Spenzer?" said Stave. "This is your territory, I think . . . '

Spenzer cleared his throat as he watched Dachron watching him. "We know that the patent papers were filed in London early on Monday the 9th of April 2007," he said. "That much is a matter of record. But what we don't know is where Tellkind was, which is where our target comes in.

"Richard Anthony is the only real friend we can find that he had," Spenzer went on, "and the only time we can be sure we know where *he* is, close to the point when Tellkind must have nearly completed his work, is one week before the filing date, March 30th."

"Why not earlier?" said Dachron. "To give me more time."

"Because the computers have worked this out as a best-case scenario," said Spenzer. "It's the only window we have open to us."

Dachron stared away into the middle distance and began snapping his fingers – *KLIK-KLIK-KLIKETY-KLIK* – as he paced up and down the room. Everyone waited silently for him to say something, watching the man who, depending on how he felt, could save the world. The Psych team had said they thought there was a 40 per cent chance, at best, that he would agree to go; there was no guaranteeing, they said, how he would respond.

"OK." Dachron stopped pacing. "Risk it for the biscuit!"

"Excuse me?" said Stave.

"I'll go."

"He must've bought it, then," said Spenzer, after Dachron had left the room with Vena and Josh.

"What?" asked Stave.

"That bunkum I gave him about this being the only window we have."

"You sounded very convincing to me."

"Yeah, well, I feel pretty bad about not telling him the truth." Spenzer screwed up the sheet of megafiche in his hand and threw it away.

"People like Dachron Amok don't need to be told the truth," said Stave, "they need to be told what to do – and *that*'s the truth, Spenzer."

"You don't think we should have told him that the override might not last much longer than the seven days, then?" queried Spenzer. "He doesn't *need* to know that this *is* a suicide mission – that there's no way back and, once the override slips, he and his 'host' are dead?"

"No, I do not," said Stave.

The Project Take-Over laboratory was a hive of activity, buzzing with nervous energy. In the middle of the large room sat an odd-looking chair – nicknamed the Ejector Seat – with a big Plexi-glass canopy cantilevered above it. Thick ropes of cable snaked away from the chair to banks of hastily assembled computer equipment, while others went out of the room to a massive power generator somewhere else in the building.

Men and women, all wearing sterile medical-style clothes, complete with face masks and synth-skin gloves, made last-minute adjustments to programs, circuitry, laser arrays and the rest of the paraphernalia that went to make up what Josh Parmar referred to as the TRiP engine: the machine that would remove the prime essence of Dachron Amok, convert it into a series of delicately moulded electrical pulses and fire them back down the time-line. Hopefully.

The man himself was in another part of the building, being given a crash course in late twentieth-century social history, with massive amounts of relevant data being downloaded straight into the appropriate parts of his cerebral cortex. He did not see the point. All he wanted to do was get on with the job. If there was one thing Dachron hated it was being bored – in reality the major factor in his decision to accept the mission had been the mind-numbing tediousness of his life as a soldier. He wanted something more exciting than cross-border clean-up operations. Project Take-Over seemed to him to be the ultimate in guerrilla missions; but he'd have the perfect disguise – only his mind would be there.

"Have we finished?" Dachron said, turning to Spenzer. "These cortex implants are itching like crazy – *inside* my head!"

"We're nearly done," said Spenzer, checking the download screens. "Anyway, they're not ready for you in the lab yet . . ."

The door to the room opened and Vena Cardoza came in. "Five minutes," she said.

Spenzer, concentrating on his work, looked puzzled. "Sorry?"

"Josh says everything's as ready as it'll ever be, and can you be upstairs in five minutes?"

KLIK-KLIK-KLIKETY-KLIK.

"Are you nervous, Dachron?" asked Vena.

"No, tired of waiting."

"Well, the waiting's over, soldier . . ."

Spenzer watched through the large plate-glass window. *He* was nervous; his stomach fluttered and he realized he hadn't felt like this since he was back at school and waiting to hear his exam results.

This was it. The moment of truth. An incredible amount of work had gone into Project Take-Over and still no one *really* knew if it was going to work or not; they were sending part of a human being – the part that actually made him human – off on a perilous voyage of adventure and discovery, with no way of knowing what the chances of success were. The whole team, apart from Dachron, who appeared not to understand the concept of tension, was in a high state of nerves; tempers were frayed and everyone was ragged from lack of sleep.

And there was Dachron, looking cool as an iced beer in a one-piece blue cotton overall, strapped into the Ejector Seat. Electrodes were attached to his hands and feet and underneath the Plexi-glass hood Spenzer could see hundreds of microfine wines that seemed to be growing out of his shaved head. It looked like he'd had a high voltage current passed through him – which, thought Spenzer, would not be very far from the truth in a few minutes' time, once the barbiturate-like hypnotic drug he'd been given had done its job. But for all that, Dachron sat there as if he was relaxing in the shade.

"Brave man," said Spenzer as Stave Barron came and stood next to him.

"To be brave you have to care what happens to you, Spenzer." Barron jerked his head at the window. "He couldn't give a damn."

Through the glass they could both hear a high-pitched whine set up and they saw all the techs hurriedly exit the room, leaving only Josh and Vena at the controls. Underneath the whine they could suddenly feel the throbbing of a deep bass pulse and then the lights momentarily dimmed.

"I thought we had our own power supply," said Spenzer, who for a moment had thought his eyes were giving out.

"We do, but I think this is testing it to the limit . . . Any moment now . . ."

The whining sound went so high it became inaudible, while the bass pulse speeded up and became a dull roar that pounded the air. Spenzer looked at Dachron. He was rigid, his hands balled into fists; then, out of the corner of his eye, Spenzer saw Josh press something on one of the control panels and Dachron's body appeared to try and leap out of the seat and his face contorted in a silent scream.

Then everything stopped. No more noise. Brighter lights. Dachron's body still as a corpse on an undertaker's slab.

"He's either dead or he's gone," said Stave.

"You don't like him, do you?" Spenzer said, staring at the glass in front of him rather than through it.

"Not really," agreed Stave. "Soldiers, by and large, create nothing but chaos . . . I hate the fact that, in this supposedly refined and civilized society, we still need their skills. A sad reflection on the human condition, wouldn't you say?"

"We'll never be perfect, Stave" – Spenzer glanced at the old man – "and there'll always be a place for people like him . . . That's just the way it is."

Stave Barron shook his head. "That's the trouble with being a scientist . . . always trying to make the world better, never being satisfied with the way it is. The cause of many of our problems, I suppose."

"At least we have a chance to put this one right," said Spenzer.

"We can only hope . . ."

6

Day 1 – Sunday, 1st April 2007. 2.45a.m.

The party was over. And what a party it had been! Steve hadn't really planned Saturday evening to turn out like it had, but then he hadn't known his parents were taking his sister away on a surprise birthday trip to EuroDisney in Paris. The whole thing had actually been a bolt from the blue for everyone. Steve's gran had won a Family Ticket in some raffle or other and only told his parents about it on Friday night.

They'd asked him if he'd wanted to come, but the last thing *he* wanted to do was spend a week surrounded by Mickey and his pals – in Florida, maybe, but on the outskirts of Paris? He didn't think so. Steve had won an immense amount of Brownie points by offering his ticket to Judy's best friend Sally. A couple of ten-year-old girls were going to have the time of their lives, and one delighted sixteen-year-old was going to get the house to himself.

His parents didn't know he'd got the house to himself, but the moment they left he'd told Nadja, their Czech au pair, she could have some extended quality time with her new boyfriend. She'd needed absolutely no persuasion, promising to come back in good time to get the place cleaned up for when his parents arrived home.

Things had kind of spiralled out of control, the way they tended to do where Steve was concerned. A couple of mates coming round for pizza, beer and a DVD or three had ended up with near on ten of them having a roaring time – making so much noise the police had turned up just after midnight and told them to turn his dad's brand new 100-watt sound system down. Always a sign you were having a good party.

The party carried on – even though Tim was violently sick and Chaz had a fight with Robbie over Charlotte and Robbie and Charlotte had left. Around two o'clock, when there was no more food or drink left and three people were already asleep in the breakfast room, Steve decided the party was over.

"Anyone who wants to stay can stay," he said. "But you *gotta* help clear up tomorrow morning."

Five weary heads nodded in unison and then dragged themselves off to find somewhere to crash. Steve went into the kitchen for a glass of water and through a mild beer haze found himself looking at a bomb-site. Half an hour later he'd cleared up just enough so it would be possible to have breakfast without too much effort.

"Bed . . ." he muttered as he stumbled upstairs and opened the door to his room, "sleep . . . dream . . . *what?*"

Someone was already in his bed, and whoever it was was snoring. Loudly.

Steve closed the door and shuffled down the corridor; if anyone was in his parents' bed he'd chuck them out and make them sleep on the floor. They weren't and so he climbed out of half of his clothes, couldn't be bothered with the rest and crawled under the blue and white, country-style gingham duvet. He was asleep in seconds.

Nightmare. A bellowing, thunderous howl filled the air. He was being chased down an endless tunnel by something monstrously, obscenely huge that was trying to smother him. His legs felt like they had lead weights attached to them and the harder he tried to run, the slower he went; he wanted to yell out, scream for help, but he couldn't; nothing worked.

The tunnel was brightly lit, but a shadow — really more of a blanket of heavy un-light, it seemed to his panicked senses — was looming over him, about to blot out everything. This weird, tormented place was nothing like he'd ever experienced before. He'd had his fair share of bad dreams, waking in a muck sweat, sitting up in bed with his eyes wide open and then being too scared to go back to sleep. He knew the feeling of bizarre unreality that pervaded dreamworlds — the half-seen faces, the skewed colours, the whispered soundtrack. But this . . . this was something else again.

There was only one way to describe it. Real.

In the middle of the madness, the demented, sucking horror, Steve somehow knew that this was *actually* happening to him. Not wishing to believe it wasn't going to help, wasn't going to make it go away, wasn't going to let him wake up and guzzle air like a half-drowned man.

If he wanted this to stop he had to do something. Fight, punch, howl, scream, kick, stamp, shriek — go berserk, with his mind as the only weapon he had.

The dark cloud touched him and he shuddered at the coldness of its probing fingers inside his head. The only thing he could think of doing was to conjure up images of searing heat, blazing, white-hot and superheated flames. He made himself think of himself as being the blistering, psychotic lunacy that was a nuclear explosion.

He vibrated with a scorching energy.

He exploded.

He hit the floor.

Steve felt like he'd been dropped from the ceiling, but realized he'd just fallen out of bed. He lay on the floor, groaning. The nightmare – which hardly described what he'd been through – was the worst he'd ever had. If he closed his eyes he could still see all the images with a frightening clarity, so he fought to keep them open, even though the light hurt.

All his senses seemed to be heightened: the smell of his mother's *Obsession* perfume pricked the back of his nose . . . he could feel individual wool fibres in the twist pile carpet . . . taste the garlic from last night's American Hot pizza. Hear noises in his head.

At first it was like a kind of post-gig deafness. A high-pitched whine rose and fell and behind it was the static crackle of a mis-tuned radio. Or was it voices? Steve strained to catch what he thought might be words of a half-remembered song but nothing sensible came out of the interference.

He was lying on his front, one arm trapped underneath him, and he tried to roll over. Pushing with his free hand he raised himself and slumped on to his back. He immediately wished he hadn't; his head lolled sideways and he couldn't bring his eyes into focus. How much had he drunk? Surely not *that* much . . .

Pinned to the floor, unable to move, Steve began to shiver uncontrollably. He forced his head round and struggled to focus on the clock by the bed. 6.30, no wonder he was cold. He slowly levered himself up into a sitting position and sat for a moment while his stomach churned, trying to decide whether it wanted to be sick or not. Apparently it didn't, so he reached over and pulled the duvet towards him, wrapping it round his shoulders.

The noise in his ears wowed and fluttered and then levelled out. Steve sat on the floor in a zombified huddle, trying to work out what to do next: should he go back to bed? Should he try and make it to the bathroom and take a couple of aspirin? Or would it be better not to risk any more movement and simply stay where he was until he felt better?

He realized he'd stopped shivering and was rocking backwards and forwards, staring into the middle distance. "Maybe a cup of coffee," he thought. "Strong, black, two sugars . . . that should do the trick."

Steve rocked forward, reached for the bed post and hauled himself up off the floor. "Boy, but my head hurts!" muttered Steve, clinging on to the bed for dear life.

"*Your* head hurts?" said a loud voice.

Steve looked round. The room was empty, the door closed. Either he was going mad or someone had slipped something highly illegal into one of his drinks . . .

7

Painful. Frightening. Claustrophobic.

They hadn't told him it would be like that – but then, Dachron had to admit, those scientific types really hadn't got the slightest idea if it would *actually* work at all. Well, it had. He certainly wasn't strapped to a chair in a room somewhere in the Jo'burg sprawl any more . . . though where he was was another matter entirely.

The transfer had been weird. That was the only word that came to mind. *Weird*. He'd never been very good with words; he felt much happier doing things and had always hated after-mission debriefs when he was supposed to report back in detail every move he'd made. There was no one to report to now, no one to tell how he'd had to fight his way through what had felt like a wall of fire. Really fight.

Dachron reckoned he must've passed out for a moment or two because he didn't feel in control of anything any more. It was like his mind was this tiny island lost in the middle of a vast ocean, unable to communicate with the rest of his body. And then he remembered . . . it wasn't his body. Is this what it feels like to be forty-seven? he thought. What a total drag.

He could see things, but nothing he saw was in focus

or made any kind of sense. And then he heard the voices, or maybe it was just *a* voice, he couldn't be sure, and he realized that stuff was happening that he wasn't responsible for. He could feel himself moving, like he was floating in oil, and the more he tried to control what was happening the more his brain felt as if it was about to explode.

"Boy, but my head hurts!" he heard a voice say.

"*Your* head hurts?" said Dachron.

Steve couldn't move. He stood by the bed, the duvet wrapped round his shoulders, swaying unsteadily. Someone was talking to him *inside* his head. He'd heard about people with multiple personalities, crazies who slipped in and out of the various characters that inhabited them. Schizophrenics, wasn't that what they were called? Types like that used to get locked up and fed on Mogadon, or whatever those heavy-duty sledgehammer drugs were called. Now they just let them wander the streets . . . don't care in the community. Is that what was happening to him? Was he going mad?

The insane thought of his parents coming home to find him wandering about thinking he was any number of other people occurred to Steve, bringing him back to the equally insane reality that he was hearing things. What do you do if you start hearing voices? Talk back?

Steve checked that he really was alone in the room, and then said, "Anyone there?"

Silence.

He breathed a sigh of relief. It was a hangover . . . he'd been imagining it all . . . everything was OK and he could go right back to bed. He'd wake up at midday feeling starving hungry and with a tongue like an old sock as if this whole thing had never happened.

"My name is Dachron," said the same voice as before. "Dachron Amok."

"Who the . . . ? Wha . . . ? But . . ." spluttered Steve; his knees gave way and he slumped on to the bed, holding his head in his hands. "I've gone skitzo," he moaned.

"Who are you?" said the voice. "What's your name?"

It was Steve's turn to go quiet. For a split second he actually couldn't remember who he was.

"Come on," said the voice. "Spit it out!"

"My name's, um . . . Steven, Steven Anthony," he said. "Steve . . . my friends call me Steve."

"Not *Richard* Anthony?" said the voice.

"No."

"Damn!"

"Hey!" said Steve, his head jerking back as the voice in his head shouted. "What am I doing? I'm talking to myself, I'm *hearing* things, I'm having conbloody-vulsions!"

He leapt off the bed, his head feeling slightly woozy, and stumbled over to his mother's dressing-table. He pulled the stool out and sat down in front of the mirrors. There was a big one, with a smaller one on each side; three of himself stared back at him.

"Oh, God . . ." he said. He looked awful; his hair was a mess and needed a wash, he had dark circles underneath his eyes and he was paler than a ghost.

"You're not forty-seven either," said the voice.

"What the *hell* is going on?" said Steve through gritted

teeth. "No, I'm *not* forty-seven, I'm sixteen and I've gone barking mad and it's not fair!"

"Calm down," said the voice.

"*Calm down?*" hissed Steve. "I must be the only crazy person who hears reasonable voices – I thought you were supposed to tell me to go out and do things . . . like murder people with red hair because it was the mark of the Devil!"

"Listen to me, Steve. You haven't gone mad, but something has gone wrong . . ."

"You can say that again!" Steve stood up suddenly, knocking the stool over. "On second thoughts, don't . . . on second thoughts, *shut up*! Go away! Leave me alone!"

He stormed across the room and yanked the curtains open, letting the early morning light flood into the room. The sudden brightness made him squint and shield his eyes. Through hooded lids he saw that the world outside looked normal enough, much like it had yesterday and the day before. Except then he hadn't realized his world was about to be ripped apart.

"Shower!" he said, spinning round, as if having one would wash him clean, outside and in.

Dachron watched and waited. This was a situation neither he nor anyone else had anticipated. Something had gone wrong, very wrong, with the transfer. He hadn't really paid too much attention to what they'd told him back in Jo'burg, technical details bored him rigid, but from what he remembered, as long as they'd zeroed in on their target correctly the Take-Over *should* have been complete.

But, from what he could work out, while the techs had managed to hit *a* target, it hadn't been the right one. The wrong Anthony had been in the frame when he'd been shot back through time – "down the ribbon", as that guy Parmar had put it – and he'd only managed to get control of *part* of him. So here he was in 2007, with only seven days to complete his mission, and the unexpected problem of a frightened, angry co-pilot to deal with.

He'd taken a good look at his new "self" when the boy – because he was really no more than that – had sat in front of the mirror. Not a bad-looking kid: brown hair, brown eyes, strong features, reasonably athletic. Certainly a better package than he'd been expecting to have to work with.

But the kid, Steve – wasn't that what he'd said his name was? – was more than a little off-balance. Hardly surprising, if you thought about it. He was feeling edgy and nervous himself and he'd been prepared for a rough landing, thought Dachron. The kid had no idea what was going on and he didn't blame him for thinking he'd gone mad. Watching him lose it in front of the mirror made Dachron think it best to keep quiet for a bit, take it easy and try to figure out what to do next.

He was stuck with the fact that he didn't have complete control of the person he was now in. No matter how hard he tried he couldn't change the reality that he was trapped – every attempt he'd made to reach out and become more dominant had failed, and he was having to come to terms with the realization that, for him to be able to do anything, he was going to have to get Steve's co-operation.

If Dachron knew anything about himself it was that he was good at playing a waiting game. In his business it had been essential. Fighting the mean, underhand dog fights that were what guerrilla warfare was made up of had meant hours, sometimes days of inaction, often in the worst of conditions. Letting the kid take a shower and calm down wasn't going to stretch his talents at all.

It was a strange feeling, letting someone else take over. It reminded him of the time he'd nearly died. A hot pursuit task force he'd been with had been ambushed; he'd taken a couple of old-fashioned vanadium-tipped rounds in his thigh and the toxins had made him completely delirious. He had almost no recollection of the rescue, or his two months in hospital, except that he couldn't *do* anything for himself. Just like now. As he'd said to himself before – weird.

Steve turned the water off and stood, dripping, in the shower. He felt better, like he'd had all the wrinkles steam-ironed out, and he was beginning to convince himself that what had happened in the bedroom was nothing more than a waking dream. He hadn't had enough sleep, was all. Pushing the door open he grabbed a towel and wrapped it round him.

Getting out of the shower cubicle he started drying himself, realizing as he did so that he was dripping all over the bathroom floor – just like his dad was always telling him not to.

"Whoops!" he said, hopping on to the mat in front of the basin. "Sorry, Dad!"

Rubbing the condensation off the mirror he examined his face, thinking he really ought to have a shave to finish the job off properly. Running the hot tap, he squirted some foam directly on to his chin and smoothed it in.

A couple of minutes later Steve was patting on some aftershave, wincing slightly and congratulating himself for not having any cuts. He looked at his watch: nearly 7.30. Time, he thought, for some breakfast and a skim through the Sunday papers – if they'd arrived. He grinned at his reflection.

"Hi," said Dachron. "Can we talk now?"

8

Day 1 – Sunday, 1st April 2007. 8.10 a.m.

Steve sat in the kitchen, ignoring the black coffee and toast he'd made without really knowing he was doing it. He wasn't hungry any more, he wasn't thirsty either. He was stunned.

For the last fifteen minutes he'd been listening to a voice in his head telling him what amounted to a huge science fairy-tale. It had to be; no way could it be true. The voice said he was someone called Dachron Amok, who came, so he claimed, from the year 2667 and had been sent back to stop the world from being destroyed by some kind of bizarre engine exhaust.

Steve had scribbled odd notes on a scrap of paper as Dachron's voice talked at him, more to give his hands something to do than anything else. Looking down he saw he'd written *2667-2007 = 660 yrs!*, *AMOK?*, and *CHARM*. The figures and words meant about as much to him as if they'd been written in hieroglyphics.

"Stop," he said. "This isn't making any sense . . . I don't care *how* you got here, what I really want to know is – why me?"

"I told you," said Dachron. "It was a mistake, it wasn't supposed to *be* you!"

"OK, so why my dad?"

"Right, one more time," Dachron said patiently. "Where I come from we use a source of power called a charm drive – don't ask me how it works, because I don't have the time to go into details. The point is that it's incredibly cheap and simple to make and everyone *thought* there was absolutely no down-side whatsoever."

"And then?"

"A major screw-up was discovered, something they told me was called sub-atomic exhaust," explained Dachron. "The charm drives had been giving this stuff off since forever, but in such incredibly tiny amounts that no one had noticed . . . until someone found atomic structures were kinda coming unglued and it's End-of-the-World time – look, Steve, I'm just repeating what they told me; I got *no* idea what it all means.

"But what it boils down to is this: the man who thought the damn thing up, some guy called Simon Tellkind, lived – lives – now, and he's a friend of your father's."

"Doesn't ring a bell."

"He's someone important," said Dachron. "He's got a connection with your father . . . but for the life of me, right now, I can't remember what it is. Transfer's really shaken my head up."

"You and me, both . . ."

"It'll come back," said Dachron. "It has to, because I'm on the clock here. In my time there are people hanging on threads, waiting to see if I've done my job."

"Job?" said Steve.

"I've got just seven short days to find Tellkind – not only find him, but actually get to him, inform him of his mistake and give him some sort of subroutine that puts his Charm Principle back on the right track."

"That's it?"

"Yeah, that's it – then I'll have saved the world."

"That simple."

"Right."

"And then you go back?"

"I wish."

"You're staying here! In *my* head!" yelled Steve, thumping the table and spilling some coffee.

"You all right, Steve?"

Steve slowly looked round to find Tim standing in the kitchen doorway, frowning at him as he scratched his head. He'd completely forgotten about his posse of house guests. "Tim!" he said. "What're you doing up so early?"

"Were you *talking* to yourself?" said Tim, ignoring Steve's question as he sat down opposite him and took a piece of cold toast and jam.

"Me? No . . . well, yes . . ." Tim looked quizzical. "I was, um, practising . . . you know, some poetry I'd written."

"You write poetry?" Tim grinned. "Didn't know that."

"See," said Steve, "you're taking the mick – that's why I keep it quiet."

"Nice work," said Dachron. "You lie like a pro."

Steve ignored him. "You OK after last night, Tim?" he asked. "Were you sick again?"

"No, I'm fine, just a bit hungry," said Tim. "Can I make some more toast?"

"Sure, bread's over there," Steve nodded at the work surface next to the sink."

"Get rid of him," said Dachron.

"Them," Steve said out loud before he'd even thought.

" 'Scuse me?" said Tim.

"Then!" Steve pointed at the kettle. "Then we can have a cup of coffee; mine's gone cold!"

"What's with you, guy?" Tim got two slices of bread and dropped them in the toaster. "You nervous or something? Had a bad night?"

If you only knew! thought Steve. If you only bloody knew!

It was well after midday before he managed to get rid of everyone. They'd all insisted on sticking around and helping to clear up the house, and trying to persuade them not to would have looked very strange indeed. Why was it you could always rely on your friends to do the *exact* opposite of what you wanted them to? One of life's great mysteries.

When he finally closed the front door he let out a huge sigh. "Thank God *that's* over . . ."

"It's only just started," said Dachron.

Steve was alone now. As alone as you could ever be with somebody else rattling round your brain and insisting that you didn't have time to sit down and read the paper.

"We've got work to do!" Dachron said.

"*We?*"

"Yeah, 'we'. The situation is, I'm stuck with you and you're stuck with me and I have a mission to complete," said Dachron.

Steve sat down on the hall stairs. "You telling me I have no choice in the matter?" he said. "What if I refuse?"

"I make your life hell," said Dachron. "I never shut up – and don't forget, this is for the *rest* of your life."

"I can't believe this is happening to me!"

"Believe it."

"It's not possible – time travel is *not* possible." Steve jumped up and went to stand in front of the big mirror by the front door. "You are a hallucination!" he shouted at his reflection. "I'm sick . . . I'm ill . . . I'm gonna go to the hospital and tell them I want shock treatment, or whatever it is they give people in my condition. *That'll* get rid of you!"

"Wait a second, wait a second . . ."

"Stop telling me what to do! Leave me alone!" Steve shouted, trying to drag himself away from the mirror and finding he couldn't do it. He was standing fifteen, twenty centimetres away from the glass, his breath misting it slightly, staring into his own eyes like he was seeing himself for the first time. A quote from some book he'd read drifted to the surface of his mind, something about the eyes being the windows of the soul, and he tried to look through the pair of brown-rimmed windows in front of him.

A cloud went across the sun, darkening the hallway, and he saw, almost in slow motion, his irises widen as they readjusted to the light.

"I am in here," said Dachron. "I *am* from the future and I *need* your help."

Steve's shoulders slumped. "Do I have a choice?"

"Of course."

"Not much of a one, though."

"No."

"Some holiday *I'm* going to have," sighed Steve. "What d'you want me to do?"

"Help me find the man."

"What was his name again?" asked Steve, finally turning away from the mirror.

"Simon Tellkind."

"Simon Tellkind . . . still doesn't mean anything," mused Steve, walking into the sitting-room and looking around. Framed family photographs lined the mantelpiece and fought for viewing space on two small tables either side of a large settee.

He went over and looked at them. All the stages of family life were there: cute baby pictures, standard school shots and studio pictures stood alongside happy-snaps of him and his sister, his mum and his dad. He suddenly missed them, even his sister, and a huge sense of loneliness spread through him; whatever happened over the next week, when they got back he'd be a very different person to the one they'd left behind.

"Can you remember *anyone* called Simon?" asked Dachron. "Anyone at all?"

"No . . . no, I can't," said Steve, frowning and shaking his head as he tried to think back. Could he be someone from when his dad was still on the force? An old school friend? And then from some tiny forgotten corner of his memory he trawled up two words. "Uncle Sy," he said out loud.

"What?"

"Don't get your hopes up," said Steve, going over to a chest-high pine cupboard and opening the doors. Inside, the shelves were lined with fake leatherbound albums, each one full of pictures and each picture carefully labelled and dated. It was his mother's hobby – more of a passion, really – and if he had any chance of finding out if "Uncle Sy" meant anything at all it would be in one of these albums.

He chose the one with a sticker saying *1991* on it and began flicking through the stiff, clear plastic-covered pages. There were hundreds of images of himself as a chubby one-year-old with two much younger versions of his mum and dad. It was hard to imagine his parents were ever those people.

"Happy baby," said Dachron.

"What's to be unhappy about when you're a kid?"

"If you're lucky," said Dachron, drawn back to a time he rarely thought of now – his own reasonably sunny childhood. The darkness of his later life, the killing runs, the adrenalin-fuelled sorties against a faceless enemy, were much more sharply focused, but somewhere in the distance he too had once been a smiling child.

Steve closed the album and pulled the next one off the shelf. Here he was, walking now, playing with the Labrador puppy that had only died two years ago and pulling faces for the camera.

"Remind me, what are these called?" asked Dachron.

"What?"

"These paper pix."

"Photographs," said Steve, closing *1992* and reaching for the next year. "Don't you still have them?"

"No, pix are stored on silchips and they're like triD," Dachron said. "You know, you can walk round them?"

"I know what 3D is . . ." Steve was turning pages, hardly seeing what was on them, when one particular picture caught his eye and he stopped. There he was, a year older than in the previous book, sitting on the lap of a serious-looking man wearing glasses with thick black frames – like the ones that dead rock star, Buddly Holly he thought his name was, wore. Though that was where the resemblance ended. Neither he nor the youngish man looked very happy about the situation.

Steve looked at the caption underneath it, written in blue biro in his mother's careful, rounded script. It said: "*Steven, aged 3¼, with Sy – Dick's 33rd birthday*". Uncle Sy.

"That's him!" said Dachron.

"How d'you know?"

"They showed me a pic they'd got from some d-base or other; he was older, but that's *definitely* the guy I'm after. He's your godfather, right?"

"Yeah, but I don't think I ever saw him again," said Steve. "Leastways, I don't remember if I did."

"That was taken, when? Fourteen years ago?"

"Yup."

"Where does your father keep his records?" asked Dachron. "He got a computer here?"

"I've got my dad's old computer upstairs in my room, but he keeps all his stuff in the office as far as I know." Steve closed the album, put it back on the shelf and closed the cupboard.

"MetroPol," said Dachron.

"How'd you know that?" Steve caught sight of himself in the glass doors of a cabinet; he looked almost shocked.

"Look, Steve, they successfully sent me back – well, *almost* successfully sent me back more than 600 years, and you're surprised I know that?"

"Yeah, well . . ." Steve grinned, feeling a tad foolish.

"So what're we waiting for? Let's go there . . ."

9

Day 1 – Sunday, 1st April 2007. 1.55 p.m.

"I can't just waltz into Dad's place," said Steve. "It's all locked up and fully alarmed!"

"Has it got print coding, or some kinda pheromone seal?" asked Dachron.

"Neither, whatever they are," said Steve. "It's got a couple of Banhams on the front door and motion sensors in the rooms – linked to the local police station. I'd need keys and two sets of code numbers to get in."

"And where might they be?"

"Jeez, *I* don't even know if there's a spare set of keys in the house, *or* whether he keeps a record of the numbers here!"

"Only one way to find out . . ."

"Right, but *after* I've had some lunch," said Steve.

"We," commented Dachron. "I feel hungry as well – but make it quick!"

"Great, I'm speed-snacking for two now . . ."

Everything he needed was in the first place Steve looked. His father had told him once that people nearly always left valuable things in the most obvious places. So he'd gone straight to the "secret" compartment at the back of the drawer in his dad's bedside table, and *hey presto!* One set of office keys and a piece of paper with two four-digit code numbers written on it.

"Where is the office?" asked Dachron.

"You mean there's something you *don't* know?"

"Cut it out."

"OK," grinned Steve. "It's on Kentish Town Road."

"Can we walk there?"

Steve shook his head. "Could do, but I'm too knackered after last night – we go by tube."

"Tube?"

"You'll see," said Steve, going to get his denim jacket.

Dachron had been shocked when Steve walked straight out of the house wearing no solar protection at all – no gloves, no cream, no wrap-round mirrored glasses or helmet. What about the UV rad? he'd asked. What about retina burn and dermal sarcomas? Steve informed him that, in April at least, northern Europe's ozone layer was still in pretty good condition. They'd be all right.

It was a five-minute walk to Archway station and Dachron hardly shut up the whole way. He was amazed by how like the holoflix he'd been shown of London it all was, but horrified by the smell and the noise. Traffic was fairly light, there weren't *that* many people on the street and Steve wondered what the future smelled – or didn't smell – of.

"You should see it on a weekday," he muttered, fully aware how careful he was going to have to be not to get caught out talking to himself.

Getting a return ticket from one of the machines, he went down the escalator. Instead of running, he stood still, looking around so that Dachron could take in the fully glory that was a Northern Line station – the screeching cogs, the wavering fluorescent lights, the rubbish and the annoyingly repetitive adverts. That shut him up for a bit.

On the platform, while they waited for a train, Steve went and stood in front of a map and let him marvel at the pretty graphics and mildly obscene graffiti, silently pointing out where they were going. A low rumble in the distance told him – but not Dachron – that a train was approaching, and he went and stood down by where it would hurtle out of the tunnel. Just for a laugh.

The rumble turned to a roar as the dirty grey carriages appeared and sped down the platform, squealing to a halt.

"What the *hell* is that?" said Dachron as the doors opened, letting a handful of passengers off and the dozen or so waiting on.

"That," whispered Steve, "is a southbound, Charing Cross line tube."

"You could've warned me," growled Dachron.

No one paid Steve the slightest bit of notice as he let himself in off the street, using one of the codes on a keypad next to the door. His father's office was on the first floor, above a solicitor's, and the stairs smelled of a particularly redolent pine disinfectant. The cleaners, he thought, must've been in the day before.

Two minutes later he was tapping the second four digits into another, similar pad inside the office. There was a high-pitched whine, he saw a red light go off and a green one flick on and they were in.

MetroPol Ltd consisted of two reasonable sized rooms, a boxroom, a tiny kitchenette and a toilet. His dad employed a full-time secretary, who worked in his office, and three inquiry agents, as he called them. They had the other office. Everywhere you looked there were filing cabinets, each one, as Steve soon discovered, packed full of files.

He looked around, frowning. "Where on *earth* do I start?"

"Why not try checking out your father's desk?" suggested Dachron.

"Or maybe look under 'T' in the filing system," said Steve, scanning the massed ranks of cabinets.

"I'd go for the computer," advised Dachron. "Where is it?"

Steve glanced down and pointed at the desktop PC set up on the desk. "There," he said. "It's brand new; he only got it last month." Dachron laughed. It was the eeriest thing, having someone else cracking up inside your own head. "What's so funny?" asked Steve.

"*That's* a computer?" said Dachron. "How does it work?"

Steve had just spotted a shelf lined with diaries that, as far as he could tell, went back ten years before he was born. "I'll show you in a minute," he said, pulling down a volume marked *1993*, the year the picture had been taken of him sitting on Simon Tellkind's knee.

Half an hour later, after cross-referring with an ancient

address book he'd found tucked away on top of a shelf, Steve had an address and a telephone number . . . that were both at least a dozen years out of date.

"Ring it anyway," insisted Dachron. "You never know."

"Never know what?" said Steve. "He's sure as heck not going to still be living there, and it's Sunday – whoever *does* live there now's likely to be out."

"Just try it."

Steve checked the directory and dialled the Watford number. As he listened to the phone at the other end ring and ring he rehearsed what he was going to say:

"Excuse me, but do you know anything about the person who used to live at this address thirteen years ago?"

It sounded ridiculous, but what else could he say? How else was he going to put it? He realized he'd been hanging on for quite some time with no reply and was about to put the phone down when he heard the tone stop.

"27816," he heard a voice say.

Five minutes later, after having spun the nice lady at the end of the line some cock-and-bull story about trying to find a long-lost relative, Uncle Sy – sort of true – he'd found out that Tellkind had sold the house in 1996, the lady *used* to have a forwarding address, but had lost it, and that even last year they'd had some post for him. Sorry for bothering you, and back to square one.

"I s'pose I'd better start hitting the filing system," sighed Steve as he put the phone down.

"Show me the computer first," said Dachron.

"OK," Steve grinned, "*any*thing not to have to start poking round in that lot."

Pushing the screen up and switching the laptop on, he waited until everything settled down, then opened up the Internet connection. A home page flashed up.

"What's that?"

"Google. See," Steve pointed at the screen, "it says."

"And a google is?"

"A search engine. We ask questions, it gives us answers . . ."

"Right," said Dachron. "We call it the Mesh. And you have to talk to it through that keypad?"

"Right."

"So talk."

"OK, OK, who's the doer here?" Steve began typing Simon Tellkind's name in.

"This stuff is so *primitive*!" said Dachron. "They told me it was going to be different, but I don't think I've even seen anything like this in a museum."

"Shut it for a moment, will you?" said Steve. "I'm trying to concentrate."

In silence Dachron watched as Steve began scouting round various web sites and university notice-boards, following paths, finding dead-ends and scurrying off down new and unexplored data trails. At some point he picked up a mention of Tellkind in a specialist scientific forum and chased him for all he was worth, ending up nearly an hour and a half later with just one piece of firm information.

Currently, the man Dachron was after lived in the small Hertfordshire town of Berkhamsted.

"That's it?" said Dachron. "No address, no phone number?"

"What you see is what we got," replied Steve, tapping the screen, "and right now I can't think of a way to find out anything else, except going there."

"So when do we leave?"

"Tomorrow. I'm going home 'cos I'm whacked," said Steve. "Pick up some nosh on the way back and veg out for the evening in front of the box. What d'you fancy? Greek, Indian, Chinese?"

"A translation."

"Eh?"

"I didn't understand a word past 'going home'," said Dachron.

10

Day 2 – Monday, 2nd April 2007. 10.30 a.m.

Steve woke up feeling almost as tired as when he'd crashed out some time before eleven the night before, and when he opened his eyes he couldn't quite remember where he was. For a couple of minutes, as he lay staring at the ceiling, he even forgot about Dachron, the time-travelling cuckoo who'd hunkered down in his mental nest.

And then he saw his hands.

They were filthy; three of his nails had been torn and those that hadn't had black dirt stuck right up underneath them. Puzzled, Steve poked his arms out from under the duvet to get a better look and realized he was wearing a shirt. Flinging the cover back he saw he was fully dressed, apart from his shoes.

He sat up, rubbing his face; he was sure he'd undressed before going to bed – he'd not been *that* tired. And his clothes were in about the same state as his hands, covered in greasy fingermarks and oil . . . just like the sheets.

"What the hell . . . ?" Steve muttered. "Dachron?"

"Yeah?" came a slow reply.

"You know anything about this?"

"About what?"

"Don't play dumb . . . look at the state I'm in!"

"*We're* in."

"I didn't need reminding," said Steve angrily. "Did you do this – and if so, how?"

Dachron didn't say anything for a short while, and then Steve heard a kind of sigh. "I'm sorry I didn't clean up . . . I'd had it by the time I'd finished and just crashed."

"Finished what?" asked Steve. "How come I don't know anything about this?"

"You were out for the count," said Dachron.

"And you?"

"I discovered something about our condition."

"I can't wait to hear what that is," said Steve. "Don't tell me – we sleepwalk and do a bit of car repair while we're at it!"

"You're parking in the right street, but outside the wrong house," said Dachron. "What happens is, once you zed out, I get complete control . . . just like they told me I'd have, if things had gone a hundred per cent right."

"I've been up all night?" Steve frowned and examined his hands. "What have I – you – been doing?"

"Making something."

"Where is it?"

"Downstairs, in the kitchen."

Steve stood in the doorway of the kitchen. It too was a mess, looking more like a workshop than a place where food was supposed to be prepared and eaten. Resting upside down on its saddle and bars in the middle of the floor was his bike, his beloved matt black Hardrock Sport Disc – a hard-earned bargain he'd recently managed to

61

get off e-Bay. All knobbly tyres, alloy frame, Shimanos and cold forged dropouts. An all-terrain bike to die for.

"What have you done?" he said. "Have you *broken* it? Have you come back 600 years just to spend the night wrecking my bike?"

"No."

"What then?" demanded Steve, his hands trembling with an ill-concealed fury at the prospect of something having happened to his bike. He calmed down slightly at the thought that, actually, he'd have to hit himself if he wanted to punch out Dachron.

"I made a few *adjustments*," said Dachron, aware that, just maybe, he should've asked before he'd gone to work. "It kinda goes faster now."

"How can it? A bike can only go as fast as the bloke pedalling can make it!" Steve said as he walked over to take a closer look. The bike *seemed* OK, he couldn't find anything obviously wrong with it. "What did you do?" he asked, picking the bike up, flipping it over onto its wheels and sitting astride it.

"Put in a charm-drive motor," said Dachron.

There wasn't a lot of traffic about. Which was lucky, really, as riding the new, improved Hardrock Sport had turned out to be quite an experience. Whatever Dachron had done – and so far he'd been abnormally silent on the subject – had added some weight to the bike, but not much. Then again, he could have bolted a couple of kilos of lead on to it and it wouldn't have made any difference. When the charm-drive kicked in it did so with a steel-capped toe.

Steve had cycled off up his street, turned left into Junction Road and pedalled towards the Archway roundabout.

"How do I make this charm thing work then?" muttered Steve; he had his iPod on and hoped that talking to himself would just look like he was singing along.

"Take the next left, up that hill," said Dachron, "and I'll tell you."

Steve curved off up the bleak Archway Road, downshifting the Grip Shift into a lower gear and standing up on the pedals as he began the long run to where things levelled off by Highgate tube.

"Sit down," ordered Dachron. "Now pull that handle in your right hand out, haul it back and hold tight!"

Steve did as he was told and found himself almost being flung off the bike by the force of the take-up. The bike shot forward, its off-road tyres – great to pose with, but by no stretch of the imagination made to hug tarmac – hissing like rain on a fire.

"*Jeez!*" he shouted as he flew up the hill and underneath Suicide Bridge, north London's premier high-dive spot for those at the low point in their life. "How do I stop?"

"Twist the grip forward and brake, like you normally do," said Dachron. "But do it *gently!*"

"How fast can this go?" yelled Steve, grinning madly at the driver of a clapped-out Sierra estate labouring away in the slow lane.

"*Slow down!*"

"Why? This is great!"

"Because someone's going to notice what you're doing,"

said Dachron. "And I seem to recall you telling me that a bike only goes as fast as the person riding it can make it?"

Steve slowed down and pretended to pedal. "You're right," he said. "Got a bit carried away."

At the traffic lights Steve turned down Shepherds Hill, planning a looping route in his head, through Seven Sisters, that'd bring him back to Tufnell Park – a ride that would, under normal circumstances, have taken him an hour, plus. Forty-five minutes later (having told Dachron he didn't care *how* desperate he was, he, Steve Anthony, was stopping for a breather and an ice-cream whether he liked it or not), he was almost home.

"You *gotta* tell me more about this charm-drive thing, Dachron," he said, coasting idly down the road. "Like where *is* it, for starters?"

"Inside the bike frame."

"*Inside* – how?"

"With difficulty," said Dachron.

Steve indicated left and turned into his road. "But what's it made of?" he asked. Slowing down as he approached the house he noticed a light-coloured Mondeo parked outside. And then he saw two men, one at the front door and the other peering in through the sitting-room window. "I wonder what they want?" he said, pulling on the rear brake.

"I wouldn't do that," said Dachron, his voice suddenly much harder.

"What?"

"Something doesn't feel right . . ."

Steve felt a weird shiver run down his neck and across

his shoulder blades. "It's just two blokes . . . isn't it?"

"Trust me," said Dachron. "In my business you listen to your intuition if you want to live, and I've got alarm bells – hit the grip and let's get outta here!"

There was something in Dachron's tone that stopped Steve from asking any more questions. Twisting his right wrist he powered the mountain bike forward and sped past his house, not stopping until he came to the T-junction with Dartmouth Park Hill.

"What do we do now?"

"Take a look at the office," said Dachron.

"Who were those people?" Steve checked the traffic and turned down the hill towards Kentish Town. "They didn't look odd to me."

"I don't know who they were, but I recognize the type," said Dachron.

"What type?"

"In my business we call them rats . . . their sort are sly, vicious gutter boys trained for dirty work," explained Dachron. "You can put them in whatever clothes you like, but their eyes give them away every time – they never stop moving."

There was no answer to a comment like that, so Steve kept quiet and five minutes later he was gliding past his father's office. Another light-coloured Mondeo was pulled up by the pavement opposite the door, and when he glanced up at the window he saw the lights were on.

"The rats are here too," said Dachron.

"What's going on," asked Steve, panic rising like mercury on a hot day.

"I got no idea," replied Dachron. "But it looks like we must've stirred up one heck of a muddy pool."

"How?"

"Can only be something we did yesterday."

"We didn't *do* anything yesterday," said Steve, accelerating the bike away.

"Yes, we did," said Dachron. "If these systems you have are anything like ours, we blazed a trail across that network of computers wide enough for a blind man to follow . . . and one thing types like this aren't is blind. If I'm right, someone's interested enough in us trying to find Tellkind to come looking."

"What now?" Steve asked shakily.

"Keep going . . . I need time to think," said Dachron. "Find somewhere where there's a lot of people."

Minutes later Steve was in the middle of the sea of people who'd flocked to Camden Market. Under any other circumstances he'd have enjoyed the loud, multicoloured hustle of what was more like a Middle Eastern souk than a north London high street.

There were people selling bootleg CDs and DVDs, others plaiting hair, touting cheap jewellery, candles, T-shirts – anything you might want, but didn't really need. The air was filled with the smells of fast food and slow cars, and amongst this jostling confusion of sales-pitches and street life Steve felt cast adrift and completely isolated.

11

Day 2 – Monday, 2nd April 2007. 1.30 p.m.

It was like Steve's whole world had been ripped apart and hastily Sellotaped back together again. Nothing quite fitted, pieces were missing and in the middle of it all was something – some*one* – that shouldn't be there: Dachron Amok.

Your mind wasn't a part of your body that normally got much attention; it was you and you were it, and that – if it was working OK – was usually all there was to it. Coming to terms with playing host to a battle-hardened guerrilla fighter from the twenty-seventh century was never going to be the easiest thing to do, especially when you had no one to talk to but yourself. And if you did that either he'd be listening or someone else'd hear you babbling and then your troubles would be doubled.

To drown his thoughts out he'd switched on his iPod and spun the wheel round to "Painful". It didn't solve any of his problems, but the thumping bass and growling guitars did lighten the load somewhat. Then, above the screaming vocals, he thought he could hear someone calling his name. Glancing around he turned the volume down.

"If you ain't deaf *we* soon will be!" said Dachron.

"I needed time to think as well," whispered Steve.

"With *that* racket?"

"You sound just like my dad."

"Thanks. Look, we've got to get out of here now," said Dachron. "It's way too hot to stick around, and now they – whoever *they* are – know we're looking for Tellkind there'll be eyes everywhere. Where was that place we found him at?"

"Berkhamsted."

"Let's go."

"Wait a second!" Steve needed to find somewhere more private to carry on a discussion like this. He saw a side-turning off the main street and wheeled the bike up it. "I've got a total of £4.97 on me right now and no way of getting any more. That's not enough to light out on a trip like this with."

A bedraggled figure lurched out of a doorway and stumbled past them towards the street. Red-rimmed eyes stared at Steve from a face beaten like an old tin plate. "Spare any change, guv?" the man asked, his cigarette voice heavy with despair, tinged with a desperate menace.

Steve gave him 50p, aware that the distance between himself and this poor empty shell of a man had suddenly got a lot closer. He couldn't go home, he had almost no money and precious few options. Begging wasn't one of them either. "You still have people like that in your time, Dachron?" he asked as the man shuffled off.

"No one's ever found a cure for losing the plot, big time."

"Can't hang around here much longer," sighed Steve, "but without any money . . ."

"What about one of your friends?" interrupted Dachron. "Those guys you threw out this morning."

"They're as broke as I am," said Steve, and then stopped as a thought occurred to him. "Ellie," he muttered, "*she* might be able to help."

"Ellie?"

"Family friend, almost like my sister," explained Steve, getting on the bike. "Her father's our doctor and I know they're around this weekend."

Ellie lived on the outskirts of Highgate in a house not unlike his own. As he approached it Dachron asked him if there was another way in so that he could keep his arrival as secret at possible.

"Why?" asked Steve.

"There's nothing like caution to keep a body breathing," came the circumspect response.

There was no pale Mondeo in sight as Steve wheeled right at the next road, and thirty or forty metres down he found the alleyway that ran behind the houses in Ellie's street. As a kid he'd spent hours playing there, but now he was creeping down it, not to hide from imaginary foes, but from a real-life potential threat. If Dachron's instincts were to be believed.

The back gate was unlocked, just as it usually was. Steve's dad had tried to get Dr Fraser, Ellie's father, to make the rear of the house more burglar-proof, but, thankfully, hadn't yet succeeded. The garden was a long one, the part he'd come into a shaded thicket of tall bushes and even taller trees under which lurked the garden shed. A perfect place to leave his bike and observe the house. His dad, he thought, had been right about them needing more security.

From what he could see there was no one about and so he trotted down the flagstone path, past Mrs Fraser's well-tended borders, to the kitchen door. To its right the French windows that led into the sitting-room were open and Steve snuck a look inside. Ellie was there – on her own – lounging on a sofa, reading magazines, eating crisps and watching TV. Couldn't be better.

Steve tapped on the glass. "*El!*" he whispered.

She looked up, puzzled, and then saw where the interruption had come from. "Steve!" she said. "Heard you had quite a night – why didn't I get an invite?"

Steve put a finger to his lips in a silent *Shhh!* and beckoned her out of the house. "I need to talk . . . in private," he told her quietly.

"What's the big secret, Steve?" Ellie asked. "You lot trash the house on Saturday night and want some help clearing up or something?"

"Nothing like that." Steve shook his head; this wasn't going to be an easy conversation, but what choice did he have? "Can we go up by the shed?" he said, turning to go without waiting for an answer.

"Slow down, Stevie boy!" Ellie laughed. "What's the rush? My dad's been asking about you this morning as well. Have you got into some trouble?"

"Your dad? Asking about me?" Steve stopped. "Why?"

"Oh, I don't know – some bloke phoned up asking if he knew where you were."

"The rats are on the move," Dachron said, and it was all Steve could do not to acknowledge his comment.

"Look . . ." said Steve, feeling as if he was about to burst with the frustration of not being able to tell Ellie the truth, "er, look, if you come with me I'll *try* and tell you as *much* as I can, OK?"

"All right, Mr Mystery," Ellie grinned, obviously eager to find out more. "I'm all ears."

Steve loped off up the path, Ellie behind him, and didn't stop until he was out of sight of the house. Taking a deep breath he turned to face her.

"So what's the big deal?" she said.

"This is *really* difficult, El." Steve chewed his lip. "There's no way I can tell you everything, mainly cos I don't believe even half of it myself, but I've got to go away for a few days and I need some money . . . anything you've got'd do."

"Plus a tent and maybe a jacket," said Dachron.

"Yeah, yeah, that's right – and a tent and maybe a jacket, if you got them," said Steve, scratching his ear distractedly.

"Are you all right?" Ellie frowned.

"Fine, why?"

"I don't know," she said, "you seem *different* somehow, not quite yourself."

If she only knew, thought Steve, trying to give her his best "normal" smile. "Look, Ellie," he said, "you're the *only* person I can trust and *you* have to trust me right now. I can't tell you what's happening, except that I need your help and you can't tell *any*one I've been here. Not a soul."

"You make it sound so dramatic, Stevie." Ellie was the only person who called him that – who was *allowed* to call him that. She reached over and took Steve's hand, squeezing it. "Of course I'll help," she said.

"You two an item?" asked Dachron.

"No!" said Steve, the reply slipping out before he could stop it.

"No what?" Ellie said, pulling her hand away.

"Nothing. Sorry, El, I got something on my mind."

"Have you taken anything you know, *weird*?"

"I know it must look that way, but honestly, I haven't," said Steve. "When this is all over I promise I'll tell you what I can – OK?"

"I'll be a minute or two," she said.

Watching her run back to the house Steve hated himself for not being able to tell her the truth, but the truth was he had no real idea why he was doing what he was doing. "Hey, you in there!" he said, sitting down amongst the remains of last year's leaves, his back against the shed.

"Me?"

"Who else."

"What?"

"Keep your trap shut while I'm talking to people or I'll blow this whole thing and end up in some psycho ward with my arms strapped to my sides – OK?"

"Deal. Sorry," said Dachron. "She is a peach, though."

Ten minutes later, just when Steve was beginning to worry that something might have gone wrong, he saw Ellie come running back out of the house. Dachron was right, she was a peach, but Steve had never ever thought of her in that way. As she came up the path, carrying an olive green haversack, he wondered how she saw him.

"Did anybody see you?" asked Steve.

"Not a soul," said Ellie. "Dad's up to his neck in paperwork and Mum's taken the dog out for a walk."

"Great!" Steve breathed a sigh of relief; at least this part of what he supposed could loosely be called a plan was working.

"All I've got is £15," said Ellie, handing him three crumpled £5 notes. "Sorry it isn't more."

"I'll pay you back as soon as I can, El." Steve put the money in his jeans pocket.

"Whenever, Stevie." Ellie dropped the haversack on the ground. "Are you *sure* you're not in trouble . . . police or anything? D'you want to talk to my dad?"

Steve couldn't find the words to describe the feelings, the confusion and – there was no denying it – fear, that he felt. He knew that talking about it would help him understand what was happening to him, but it would take time . . . and time was something he didn't have. He saw Ellie looking at him, puzzled by his silence; he shook his head and looked away.

"I can't . . . you know . . . talk to anyone right now," he said.

"Ask what's in the bag," said Dachron.

Steve pointed at the haversack at his feet. "What've you brought me?" he asked.

"Oh! Right . . ." Ellie knelt down and opened it. "There's that tent/sleeping-bag combo I got last year, a jumper, some spare socks and a nylon poncho. I put in a packet of biscuits as well."

"You star!" grinned Steve, squatting down with her to look.

"When will you be back?"

"I don't know . . . soon . . . I'll call you as soon as I know."

Ellie leaned over and kissed him lightly on the cheek. "Be careful," she said, and stood up.

"Yeah," nodded Steve, still looking at the haversack. "I will."

12

Day 2 – Monday, 2nd April 2007. 3.15 p.m.

"Why are we on this smaller road?" asked Dachron. "That one over to the right looks a lot faster."

"That's the MI," said Steve. "It's a motorway and bikes aren't allowed on it – even if they can go as quick as this one."

They were on the A41, speeding towards Bushey. Steve had no idea exactly how fast they were going, but if the raised eyebrows on the drivers of a couple of cars he'd passed were anything to go by it was quite a lick. He wished now that he'd thought to take his cycling helmet and fake Oakley glasses with him, but he hadn't, and there was no going back for them now. Up ahead he saw the distinctive jam-sandwich paint job of a panda car and slowed down to a more bike-like speed.

"What's the problem?" asked Dachron. "You can't be getting tired."

"The law," said Steve, keeping well over to the left of the road.

"Where?"

"In that white car with the stripes," muttered Steve, eyes on the two figures in the Astra. "That's one motor I can't pass."

The panda car stayed put at a steady pace and Steve

hung back. The situation remained unchanged for a couple of miles and then Steve realized that if the driver spotted him keeping up what must be around 30 miles per hour for that long he'd get suspicious. He switched the charm-drive off and began pedalling, falling further and further behind the white Astra.

"Take a side-road and overtake him," suggested Dachron.

"I thought of that," said Steve. "Too risky, though – what if he caught me up again?"

Up ahead he saw the Astra's left indicator start flashing and the brake lights flare as the panda car slowed to turn off the main road.

"Power on!" said Dachron, and Steve pulled the grip out and twisted it towards him.

Steve had just gone under the M25 flyover outside Kings Langley, and was going a fair lick along the road, when he realized he'd zipped past someone in uniform who'd tracked him with some kind of hand-held object. It took him precious moments to figure out that he'd gone though a speed trap, caught red-handed by radar. In front of him, as the road curved to the left, he could see a parked police car and someone getting out of it.

"Damn!" he swore, searching for a way off the road. "I've had it now . . ."

"What?" said Dachron.

"How'm I going to explain speeding on a bike, eh?" said Steve, slowing down. "And I'm trapped on the road – no way out!"

"Accelerate!" yelled Dachron. "They won't be expecting that."

It seemed like the craziest idea, but, thought Steve, what had he to lose? if he was going to be hauled up for speeding he may as well give it all he'd got. Winding the grip back he hung on for dear life as the bike did a spectacular wheelie and he all but flew by the waiting traffic cop. Risking a swift glance over his shoulder he saw the man do a hysterical double-take and then run back to his parked Vauxhall.

"He's going for a chase!" Steve said through gritted teeth, crouched down low over the straight handlebars.

"Well, give him one!" said Dachron.

"I'd rather lose him," Steve grunted, hearing the sound of a siren beginning to wail behind him. Coming up rather too fast for comfort he could see a sharp left-hand turn. Knowing he had to get off the main road if he was to have any chance of getting away, Steve slowed, braked and jumped the kerb. The Piranahpros dug into the grass, more in their natural element now they were off the tarmac, and Steve powered the bike across to the side-road.

He came off the grass and hit the blacktop again, the back wheel chasing away as it tried to grip. Steve dropped gears like a bad juggler and skidded the bike round and back on course . . . on the wrong side of the white line. The charm-drive picked up speed and he was feeling pretty pleased with himself when he saw a car coming right at him, lights flashing and horn blaring.

Swerving out of the way, but only just in time, Steve

caught the tail-end of an abusive tirade from the driver who'd so nearly mown him down. The siren was getting nearer, he still wasn't out of sight and he didn't know how much longer he could keep this kind of pace up – he was bound to make a mistake sooner or later and end up wrapping himself round something rigid. That was when he saw the signpost for a footpath.

"Here goes nothing," he said, checking the road ahead. It was clear, and as he came level with the entrance to the footpath he pulled the front brake, swung the bike round 90 degrees, its tail in the air, and the moment the back wheel hit the ground he yanked the grip back and shot off the road and down the narrow gap between two houses.

"Neat driving," said Dachron.

"Thanks," said Steve, skidding to a halt out of sight of the main road. He was sweating like a pig, more from panic than anything else. "I think it might be an idea to keep off the main roads for a bit, don't you?"

"Why not?" replied Dachron, the police car's siren *NEE-NAW*ing away into the distance.

Less than an hour later Steve found himself coasting down a long hill that eventually took him, after a major detour through a series of drab housing estates, into Berkhamsted. He'd taken things pretty easily, not pushing it, and had had an uneventful run, hardly meeting any traffic. He wondered what kind of report the police patrolmen would make – if they dared make one at all. A bike rider breaking the 50 m.p.h. speed limit would, after all, make very strange reading.

"So how are we going to find Tellkind?" asked Dachron. "We don't have an address."

"Let our fingers do the walking," said Steve.

"Translate."

"Look him up in the phone book."

"Why didn't we do that yesterday, in your dad's office?"

"I forgot, OK?" said Steve. "But there'll be one here. I can do it now, no sweat."

There wasn't. Not one single phone directory in any of the phone boxes he checked. How could he have forgotten they didn't have them any more?

"I've screwed up," sighed Steve.

"Does everyone have these books?" asked Dachron.

"Yeah, why?"

"Just go and ask, then," said Dachron. "Sooner or later someone's gonna say 'yes', aren't they?"

Amazingly enough, he was right. The friendly owner of a tobacconist shop let Steve use the well-thumbed phone books she kept under the counter. A few moments of hurried searching and Steve's finger stopped underneath the name *Tellkind, S., 62 Cowper Road*. He almost let out a cheer, but instead he bought a couple of chocolate bars and asked for directions to the address he'd found.

It wasn't very far away and Steve didn't bother using the charm-drive to get there. Pedalling slowly up the road checking the houses, he spotted number 58 and got off, pulling the bike up on to the pavement and wheeling it along.

"What do we do if he isn't in?" he muttered.

"Ask around," said Dachron.

Steve had stopped by the gate to 62, leaning his bike against the wall, when a man with a small terrier on a lead came out of the next house and walked down his front path.

"You going to see Simon?" he asked.

"Uh . . . yes," Steve nodded.

"Give him these, will you," said the man, holding out some letters. "They were in with my post on Saturday and I've been meaning to take them round all weekend."

"No problem," said Steve, taking the half-dozen envelopes, smiling.

"Thanks," said the man, walking off down the street, the dog hauling on the lead.

"OK," Steve took a deep breath, "here we go . . ."

Pushing the gate open he went up the short concrete path, noticing that one thing Simon Tellkind certainly wasn't keen on was DIY. Weeds grew everywhere and the house looked like it could do with a lot more than a simple lick of paint. Although even that would have helped. Climbing the three steps to the front door, Steve pushed the button at his eye level. Inside the house he could hear a bell ringing, footsteps approaching down the hallway.

He stood back down a step as the door opened and he saw an ordinary-looking man in his mid-thirties, wearing a grey suit, standing in the gap. It wasn't Uncle Sy.

"What d'you want?" he asked brusquely, his eyes flicking from Steve's face to the letters in his hand.

Before Steve had a chance to answer, a voice from

somewhere in the house called out and the man turned away, asking for whatever had been said to be repeated.

"He's got a gun!" Dachron's words hissed like a snake in Steve's head. "Get outta here!"

Steve's stomach did a back-flip, his eyes caught sight of the dull black pistol grip nestling under the man's armpit and his feet refused to move.

"Now!"

Steve whirled round and leapt down the path, the letters scrunched up in his fisted hand. He took the gate like it was a hurdle and grabbed the bike, swinging it round and jumping on, his heart beating so hard he thought his ears would pop. Behind him he could hear someone shouting – someone he knew had a gun. Would they shoot him in broad daylight? He knew the papers were always saying that England was becoming more like the States every day, but surely . . .

Kicking the thought away, Steve hurled the bike forward, down the road towards the High Street, its knobbly back tyre spinning madly before gripping the asphalt. He had to find somewhere out of sight, somewhere to hide so he could think what to do next . . . and very possibly shout at the damn hitchhiker in his brain.

In one day he'd been forced out of his own home, chased by the police and come face-to-face with some guy carrying a gun! Stirring up a hornets' nest would seem like a picnic after this . . .

13

Day 2 – Monday, 2nd April 2007. 4.55 p.m.

Steve was sitting on the tow-path, hiding under a bridge over the canal that ran through the town, his bike leaning against the old Victorian brickwork next to him. He hardly knew how he'd got there, he'd been in such a panic; he remembered flying down the road into the High Street, narrowly missing a car, and thought he might well have jumped the lights as he turned left past a fishmonger's – the heavy, damp smell of the shop still lingered in his memory.

He'd been speeding away from the High Street when the road did a tight switchback past a couple of shops and he'd had to slow down. That's when he saw the steps leading off the pavement and, as he'd discovered, down to the canal. It was a perfect place to hide and get his breath back, out of sight, but still able to see things. Diagonally across the canal, past the three new waterside houses, he could see the station.

"Maybe I should get the first train back to town," he muttered out loud, forgetting there was someone listening.

"Open the letters before you do that," said Dachron.

"D'you still *have* letters in 2667?"

"No."

"So how'd you know about them, then?"

"You don't think they sent me back here without some deep background, do you?"

"Oh . . ."

"So open them," Dachron repeated his request.

"But they're private!" said Steve.

"Back in my time the unit I was in was called the Devil Drivers." Dachron sounded oddly thoughtful as he spoke. "The name, so army legend has it, came from some old saying: *'He needs must go that the devil drives'*. It was our unit's motto and we always went like we had a horde of them on our tail . . ."

Steve waited, but Dachron remained silent. "So?"

"So we got the devils out there again and we need to know everything we can to get this job done," explained Dachron. "There might be something we can use in one of those letters!"

Steve looked down at the half-dozen crumpled envelopes on the ground next to him. "He needs must go," he said, picking one up, "so here goes . . ."

Two envelopes were junk mail offering time-share holidays and membership to a historical book club; three were bills – one, from the electric company, was a red reminder; and the last was a letter from the Administrative Office of something called FPC, whatever that meant. It was a terse notification that, for his records, S. Tellkind should note that his health care cover had recently been changed from BUPA to NPA.

"So much for finding loads of helpful information," sighed Steve, chucking the letter away.

"Pick it up!" said Dachron.

"What?"

"You didn't look at it properly."

Steve picked up the FPC letter and smoothed it out. "I can't see anything else," he said, scanning the A4 sheet, taking in the bold, almost 3D logo in the top right-hand corner, the three lines of typing and the scrawled signature of someone called G. Swanson (Mrs).

"Look at the bottom," instructed Dachron, "by the address . . ."

Steve scanned the line of small type that ran along the bottom of the letter. "FPC . . . Future Power Corporation," he said quietly. "So *that's* what it stands for."

"Look at the tag line, underneath their logo."

"*Energy for the New Millennium,*" read Steve.

"Interesting, huh?" said Dachron. "And check out the address."

"They're based in Berkhamsted."

"I think we should go and scope the place out."

"But what about the people at Tellkind's house?" Steve stayed on the ground, even though he could feel Dachron willing him to get up and move. "Won't they recognize me? I stick out a bit, with this rucksack."

"Carry it in front, on the handlebars," suggested Dachron, "and take your jacket off and put on the jersey the delightful Ellie gave you."

"Will you stop going on about her?" said Steve, getting up.

"Pardon me for breathing!"

"*You* don't do the breathing, *I* do."

"Thanks for reminding me," said Dachron. "And you're right about not wanting those guys at the house to recognize you . . . I don't know who they are, but they sure didn't look like house guests to me. Your police don't carry guns as a rule, do they?"

"No."

"So it looks very much like Tellkind's got himself mixed up with some pretty murky characters," said Dachron. "And I wonder what the reason for that is? What have the boys behind Future Power got to hide?"

"But he's just a scientist," said Steve as he dug out the jersey.

"You can tell a lot about a person by the company they keep – or in Uncle Sy's case, the company that looks like it's keeping him."

Steve didn't say a word for a long time. Events had gone at such a pace that it staggered him as he reran them; it wasn't just the unbelievable reality that he now shared his consciousness with another person – that in itself was something which could drive you right over the edge if you thought about it too much – but he was also involved in a clandestine battle against people straight out of the type of pulp spy novel his dad liked to read.

If he believed that Dachron Amok was really who he said he was, then he had to believe that if he didn't help him find Simon Tellkind the world would be destroyed. In six hundred years' time. That was like him going back to the 1300s and trying to convince somebody of the same thing.

The poor sucker back then would have been convinced he was possessed by demons, might well have been burnt at the stake if he'd said anything. If *Steve* said anything they'd probably lock him up, and although he didn't believe he was possessed by a demon, he didn't know how he was going to cope with sharing the rest of his life with another personality. That was such a huge concept he couldn't deal with it, dismissing the train of thought and bringing himself back to the job in hand – surviving the next few days.

Why didn't he just tell Dachron to take a mental hike? Why should he risk his life for people who didn't even *exist* yet – what possible reason was there? He wondered what his dad would do, under the same circumstances. His father was such a stickler for duty, doing what was right and proper. He'd never *really* left the police force, just set up his own little version of it when he'd retired early. His dad would no doubt say he had no choice, and, no matter how hard he tried to think otherwise, Steve realized he was right. As usual.

"You still there?" asked Dachron.

Steve was letting the charm-drive take him slowly up a hill just outside the town. "Yeah . . . why?"

"There's a sign up ahead, says FPC on it," said Dachron.

About 100 metres down the road Steve saw the large board announcing to the world that this was FPC's headquarters.

"I see it – what d'you want to do now?"

"What's the time?"

"Just after six," said Steve, glancing at his watch.

"We should find somewhere to hole up for the night," said Dachron. "Somewhere we can watch without being seen."

Steve braked and took a look around in the failing light; the FPC building was off to his right behind some bushes and a high chain-link fence; on the other side of the road he could see a building site where a couple of new houses were under construction.

"No windows, but at least the roof's on," said Steve. "How about in there?" he asked, pointing at the half-completed buildings.

"Good idea," said Dachron.

Steve wheeled the bike over the broken, muddy ground that would eventually be a front garden, but was now more like a battlefield. It was littered with rubble, pieces of gash timber and piles of bricks under plastic sheeting; in the two-car garage to one side of the nearest house he could see a cement mixer and a stack of plasterboard leaning up against a wall. He was always amazed at the way so much stuff was left lying about unattended in places like this.

Heaving the bike up over the high front door sill, Steve had just got out of sight when he heard a car coming up the road. Quickly moving down the hallway he pushed the bike into the first room he came to and went to the window. Standing in the shadows he saw yet another (maybe the same?) pale Mondeo appear round the bend in the road.

"The rats?" he said.

"Looks like it, doesn't it?" agreed Dachron.

"The man next to the driver looks like the bloke with a gun," said Steve, "the one at Simon Tellkind's place."

"I see him."

"Can't make out the other two properly."

"Doesn't matter," said Dachron. "What matters is that we're on the right track."

"What do we do now?" Steve said, watching the car turn into the FPC entrance and disappear from view.

"Wait."

"Is that it?"

"Nothing else we can do," said Dachron. "In this game waiting's more than half of what it's all about."

"Why?"

"Because we aren't the ones doing anything. You understand the difference between pro-active and re-active?" he asked.

"No, not really . . ."

"Pro-active is making things happen, re-active is responding to things that *have* happened," explained Dachron. "These guys are making the running – turning up at your house, your father's office, being at Tellkind's house. All *we* can do right now is follow them and see where that leads us."

"Does that mean staying up all night?" Steve was beginning to feel not only hungry but very tired. It had been a long, long day.

"You rest, eat something," said Dachron. "You can even get some shut-eye. I'm feeling fine."

Steve was opening up the haversack when Dachron

said this. He stopped and sat back on his heels. "I sleep and you stay awake and do stuff. How the hell does that work, Dachron?"

"Don't ask me," he replied. "I know you're spooked by what's happened to you – and I gotta say you've been a stand-up type, hope I'd've been as cool the other way round – but look at it from my side of the tracks. Things have *not* gone the way they were supposed to. I thought I might die in transit, I *didn't* think I was going to be doing a double act with someone else.

"They told me – if it worked – I'd have complete control, total override, of my own person . . . The situation I'm in now is like being in a coma. I can see, hear, feel, but I can't *do* anything . . ."

"Unless I'm asleep," Steve butted in.

"Yeah, weird, huh?" said Dachron. "Anyway, I s'pose I should apologize for screwing up your life, but it's not my fault and we're both going to have to live with it."

"For ever," said Steve quietly. He opened up the haversack and started taking things out. Underneath the sleeping bag he found Ellie had packed some salami, sliced cheese and a couple of bread rolls. The girl thought of everything. Along with the chocolate bars he'd bought at the newsagent's he had the makings of a reasonable meal. Not great, but reasonable.

"Nothing's for ever, Steve," said Dachron. "Not a damn thing . . ."

14

Day 3 – Tuesday, 3rd April 2007. 6.06 a.m.

Steve had turned in some time around 8.30. He'd found some polystyrene packing sheets which he used as a mattress, took his trainers off and zipped the bag up around him. He was asleep in seconds.

But he'd spent a disturbed night, plagued by anxious, panicky dreams, and woke feeling cold and jittery. Through bleary eyes he tried to focus on his watch, the digital read-out refusing to make sense for a second or two. Early morning light was streaming through the large unglazed hole in the wall and he felt less like getting up than ever, which was saying something.

"*Six* o'clock!" he groaned, when he finally managed to read the time, and then he noticed that not only were his trainers in a different place to where he'd left them the night before, they were now covered in fresh mud. "What the hell . . .? Dachron?"

"Yup."

"Where've I been?"

" 'Scuse me?"

"Don't give me that – you've been up to something," said Steve. "What?"

Dachron's voice, which, when he spoke, appeared to be *right* in the middle of his head, remained silent for a moment. Then: "I went into Future Power," he said, "for a recce."

"You did *what*?"

"Couldn't just lie around here doing nothing," said Dachron. "I was very careful we – you – didn't get caught."

"So what did we – you – see?" asked Steve, sitting up and stretching.

"Not 'what'," said Dachron, "more like 'who'."

"OK, so *who* did you see?"

"Simon Tellkind."

If Steve hadn't already been sitting down he would've had to. "You found him? You mean this is all over now?"

"Yes . . . and no."

"Wha . . .?"

"Yes, I found him – or at least *saw* him," interrupted Dachron. "And no, it's not all over because I didn't actually get to talk to him."

"So we're back to square one then," said Steve.

"Don't be such a downer," said Dachron. "The up-side is we know where he is now."

"But what do we do *now*?" said Steve, unzipping the sleeping bag and shivering. "Don't tell me – we wait."

"On the button . . . can't do anything else at the moment."

"I *gotta* have a pee, and that can't wait." Steve got up, stuck his feet in his trainers and wandered off towards the rear of the house.

The back garden was another churned mess, if anything worse than the front of the house. Steve stepped out and looked around; there was no one to be seen, not a sound anywhere; walking over to a trench he unzipped his jeans and let rip, watching the steam rise in the cold air. In the early morning silence – nothing moving, not another person in sight – Steve realized that this was as alone as he was ever going to get from now on. Some thought.

His stomach rumbling, he went back into the house. Scuffling the soles of his trainers on the rough concrete floor, not really looking where he was going, Steve walked into the room where he'd slept. He was about to ask Dachron what he'd been up to while he slept when he found himself staring at a man. He was in partial silhouette, small, stocky, wearing a ratty bobble hat and a thick, vinyl-shouldered donkey jacket.

"And who're you, Sunny Jim?" he asked.

Five minutes later Steve was holding a large chipped mug of the hottest, sweetest tea he'd ever burnt his tongue on. He was standing in the "kitchen" watching Ron, who turned out to be the foreman of the brickies building the house, rustle up a couple of brick-sized bacon sandwiches. He'd lit a battered portable gas stove and was frying the thick rashers in a blackened, dented aluminium pan; the smell was making Steve salivate like crazy.

"So you've not run away from home, then?" Ron looked over his shoulder at Steve. He hadn't shaved; gingery stubble, flecked with white, covered his chin, and his face was deeply lined around his eyes and mouth. The man, thought Steve, obviously laughed a lot.

"No . . . no, I haven't run away," said Steve. "I'm on my

Easter holidays and just took off to do a bit of cycling."

"How'd you end up here?" Ron used an old screwdriver to spear a couple of pieces of crisped bacon and lift them on to the waiting slices of buttered bread.

"I needed somewhere to sleep," replied Steve, "and this looked like a good place. Didn't think anyone'd mind."

"I don't mind one bit, lad . . . as long as no one's out there worryin' about you – your mum or whatever," said Ron, handing Steve a completed sandwich.

"You're going to *eat* that?" said Dachron.

"Yes – I mean thanks, Ron," said Steve, taking as big a bite as he could so he wouldn't be able to do anything for a while but nod or shake his head. He followed Ron back to the front room and helped him pull a couple of trestles up near the window to sit on.

"Ask him about Future Power," said Dachron.

Steve took another bite of his sandwich and then a swig of tea, just to let Dachron know he wasn't there to jump every time he told him to do something. Then he put his mug down on the floor. "What's that place opposite all about, Ron?"

"You mean the Effin' Poncy Creeps?"

"Eh?" Steve frowned.

"FPC," said Ron, "that lot across the road. We don't like 'em – stuck-up bunch, if you ask me. Even the security blokes treat us like dirt."

"Security?" said Steve.

"Place is tied up so tight you wouldn't believe it. Couple of my boys say they've seen blokes with guns – not 12-bore huntin' stuff, machine pistols one said he saw." Ron took a small tin out of his coat pocket and started to roll a cigarette. "Whatever they're doin' in there, they don't want anyone to know a damn thing about it, and that's for sure."

"So what *is* going on then?"

"Some kind of research, innit? Like the name says, somethin' to do with power." Ron flicked an ancient Zippo and lit his thin stick of a cigarette. "Nuclear, probably, the way they're carryin' on."

"How long have they been there?" asked Steve.

"Couple of years, I s'pose, not really sure," said Ron, flicking some ash away. "I haven't lived here that long – anyway, why're you so int'rested?"

"No reason." Steve looked out of the window, thinking he'd better change the subject. "Just saw a couple of cars go in last night and wondered what the place was, that's all."

"Right." Ron got up. "You want another cuppa before the others arrive?"

"No thanks." Steve shook his head. Even with two heaped spoons of sugar the strong reddish-brown tea had a distinctly metallic taste – one mug was definitely enough.

Ron had just gone out of the room, when Steve heard a faint beeping noise coming from his haversack. "What's that?" he whispered.

"The rats are on the move," Dacron replied.

"How'd you know?"

"Can't tell you now, but pack all your stuff up and get ready to leave!"

"Now?"

"Yeah, now."

Steve was just stuffing the sleeping bag back into the haversack when he heard the sound of a motor accelerating. He peered over the edge of the brickwork and saw a card – one of those Mondeos again – pull out of the FPC entrance and drive away down the road, back towards the town. Steve just managed to catch sight of the profile of a figure in the back seat. Simon Tellkind, he was almost sure of it.

"There he goes," said Dachron.

"Are you off then?" said Ron, coming back, mug in hand.

Steve grabbed the haversack and stood up, looking at his watch. "I'd better," he said, wondering what he'd say if Ron asked about the soft, insistent beeping. "Got a way to go today . . . North, I'm going north," he added.

"Nice to've met you." Ron put out a large, grimy hand. "You come back this way, pop in and say hello."

Steve shook his hand, nodding. "I will, Ron, thanks."

As he wheeled his bike out of the house a van that must have once been a pristine white, but was now filthy and rusty, screeched to a halt, half on the road, half off. Steve could hear the handbrake being hauled up and watched as a motley crew of builders, all dressed much like Ron, got out.

"See you, Ron." Steve waved as he walked away, the beeping noise masked by the new arrivals. Leaning against the outside of the house he noticed an old sports bike – Ron must have ridden to work on that, which was why he hadn't heard him arrive.

"OK, lad," Ron nodded. "Take care."

Take care, thought Steve as he got on the Hardrock Sport and cycled off. Yeah, he'd certainly have to do that, no doubt about it. Whoever Simon Tellkind was mixed up with didn't play games – he was up to his neck in something *really* serious. He had the feeling that this was what it must be like to have a tiger by the tail. If he let go he'd be pounced on, if he hung on who knew where he'd end up?

"What the *hell* have you got me into, Dachron?" he said.

"A bucket of trouble, Steve . . . one great big bucket of trouble."

15

Steve was sitting on a grassy verge eating a bag of crisps he'd bought. He'd had to stop cycling as he couldn't do that and listen at the same time without doing something terminal to himself on the bike. On the ground beside him was a small, calculator-sized thing, half of which was taken up with an LCD screen showing a crude map. It was beeping as a dot moved along a line marked "M1", and Dachron was explaining how come it was in his possession . . .

"That guy, Ron, was right," he said. "The place was surrounded by an electrified fence, infrared cameras, motion detectors . . . the lot."

"How'd you get in then?"

"It was pretty basic stuff, primitive compared to what I'm used to," said Dachron. "I scouted the perimeter, figured out what they had and went back and got some wire, rubber gloves and a few tools – I'd found a weak spot in their defensive layout . . ."

Steve listened, with a strange sense of detachment, to what his body had done while his mind had been asleep. Dachron told him how he'd bypassed the electrical fencing at a point where the cameras and sensors were badly aligned and snuck into the grounds. Sloppy lighting had allowed him to get close to the main building, where his behind-the-lines military training then enabled him to get into the place itself.

It was late by now, past midnight, and the place had been empty. What Dachron had wanted to do was find a way to tag the car they'd seen going into FPC – the very one he'd found, unlocked, in a car park on his way in. He was, he told Steve, amazed at how damn *amateur* these people were. Dangerous, but still amateur.

As he described the shadowy corridors down which he'd gone, the darkened rooms he'd crept in and out of, Steve felt himself go cold, the hairs on the back of his neck rising as his temperature fell. Dachron's voice was calm and so matter-of-fact, completely at odds with the way Steve felt – but then he'd never done anything like this, while for the man in his head it was a way of life.

Dachron took him through the silent building to the heart-stopping moment when, in a room marked "Security Stores", he'd had to hide under a desk as two men came in and got some equipment. In his mind's eye he was there, crouched and frozen with panic, under the cheap piece of wooden furniture, listening to the men chat.

"What would've happened if I'd woken up?" he asked.

"We probably wouldn't be sitting here now," replied Dachron.

"What did you do after they left?"

"Carried on searching until I found what I was looking for."

"That?" said Steve, nodding at the small black unit next to him.

"That, and the transmitter I put on the car on the way back out."

Steve watched the traffic whiz by in either direction. So many cars, so many people in them going everywhichway all the time; he lived in a world where the journey seemed to have become almost more important than the destination itself.

"How did you know Tellkind would be leaving in that particular car this morning?" asked Steve, bringing himself back.

"I didn't," said Dachron. "I didn't even know he was there until *after* I'd stuck the tag on. I'd just attached it—'

"How?"

"Magnet."

"Oh, right . . ."

"I was on the ground, half under the car, when a door opened and three people came out," Dachron continued. "I could only see their legs to start with, but I could hear OK. They were arguing, at least one of them was, saying he didn't like what was happening, wanted to go home, be left alone to get on with his work.

"As they came into view, walking over to another building, I could see two men, one on each side of the third, shouldering *him* forward. It was Simon Tellkind, I saw him look round – he seemed angry, scared even. And one of the guys with him was the man at his house yesterday."

"D'you think they've kidnapped him?" asked Steve.

"I don't think so. That letter we had kinda proves he

works for them," said Dachron. "I have a feeling all this is probably down to us . . . We seem to have stirred things up around him, and, for whatever reason, the guys in charge are getting heavy. He's invented something and I think they want to stop anyone else finding out – and what we've done is spooked them into moving Tellkind out of sight."

"Hadn't we better get after him then?" asked Steve.

"Doesn't look like they're moving too fast."

Steve glanced down at the tracker and saw that the dot was almost static on the screen. "Traffic jam on the motorway – rush hour going into London," he said, standing. "Super Bike should catch up in no time!"

"We don't want to get too close," said Dachron, as Steve pocketed the tracker.

"Don't worry. Until we get to the outskirts of London we'll be on completely different roads . . ."

How he was able to be so calm about things Steve had no idea. The situation he was in was so surreal, so dreamlike, that he couldn't quite take it seriously. *He* hadn't broken into the FPC place, Dachron had; *he* hadn't nearly been caught red-handed or had to creep out past sensitive high-tech security equipment, Dachron had. And although he was following a car driven by armed men, all they were to him right now was an electronic blip on a tiny screen. Not real at all. Certainly not as real as dealing with the mid-morning traffic on the North Circular Road.

Checking the tracker as he rode the bike wasn't the easiest of jobs and Steve kept on having to stop to see what the car was up to. Even so, he missed the point where they turned south down the Great Cambridge Road and had to double back through a maze of sidestreets until he too was once again on the right track.

He'd then found he'd had to slow down considerably, for fear of catching the car up, as the traffic through Tottenham, Stamford Hill and Stoke Newington was going at its customary snail's pace, while a bike – especially one with a charm-drive – sailed on unimpeded. And then the car turned east. Following, Steve saw signs for the Blackwall Tunnel coming up and knew this meant one of two things – either they were going south of the river, or the destination was Docklands.

It was Docklands.

Waiting at a red light, Steve furtively checked the tracker and saw that the blip had stopped flashing and was still in the same place it had been five minutes previously. "The eagle has landed," he muttered, putting the unit back in his pocket.

"Say what?" said Dachron.

"They've arrived," he said as the lights turned green and he set off again.

"Any idea of where it is?"

"None – the scale's too small, no real detail," said Steve. "All I can tell is that they're about a mile in front of us. I need to have a look at an *A–Z.*"

"That a map or something?"

"Every London street," said Steve.

"How do we get one?"

"Can we discuss this in a minute?" Steve was trying to

read the traffic flow and scan the road signs at the same time. "If I mess this up, next thing you know, we'll be in Greenwich."

"Bad move?"

"Totally."

Slowing to a halt, Steve got off the bike and stretched, easing the muscles in his shoulders and legs. He wasn't tired from the riding, but felt stiff and stressed-out from the tension. Looking up and down the street he searched for signs of a newsagent's or a stationer's that might sell him an *A–Z*, but couldn't find any. He was just about to get back on the bike and ride off again when he noticed, diagonally opposite him, there was a café. Parked outside it were an assortment of dirty motorbikes and cycles.

A few doors away he saw a sign above a shopfront that said *Greased Lightning Messenger Services*. Wheeling the bike with him he crossed the road.

"Where're you going?" asked Dachron. "I thought you were looking for a shop?"

"If anyone's got a street map," he said, kneeling down to lock the front wheel to a nearby lamppost, "someone in that caff will."

Taking the haversack off and slinging it back over one shoulder, Steve walked across the pavement to the café. All the windows were steamed up, and as he got nearer the smell of deep fried everything hit his nose.

I bet they don't make a bacon sarnie like Ron does, he thought to himself as he opened the door and went inside.

16

Day 3 – Tuesday, 3rd April 2007. 12.45 p.m.

It was lunchtime and the place was heaving – noisy, smelly and cramped, it was full of the kind of people who rode bikes for a living. Metal glinted from pierced ears, noses and lips; hair, cut ultra-short on top, hung in ribboned dreadlocks halfway down backs, and tattoos were visible on body parts not covered by scarred, dull black leathers. Those were, anyway, the customers who stuck out from the crowd, the ones that staggered Dachron into almost total silence as Steve joined the queue to give his order.

"Who *are* these people?" he said, his hushed whisper hanging inside Steve's head. "They never showed me anything like *this* before I left . . ."

Steve didn't bother to answer, didn't want to hear about how he was wasting time when they should be on the move. He was hungry and busied himself reading the menu, hand-painted in red on a large piece of white Formica that hung above the counter at the back. Once he'd decided on a sausage sandwich, to go, he waited to be served by the middle-aged lady with bottle-blonde hair and a voice like a klaxon.

"She's not on the menu, ducks!" the woman bellowed, cackling. "What'll it be?"

Steve stopped staring at the Page 3 calendar pinned to the wall next to him, blushed and gave his order.

"Waitress'll bring it to you," said the woman. "Next!"

Steve looked for somewhere to sit down and wait. There were three spare chairs, but two of them were at tables with people who didn't look at all approachable. The third one wasn't all that much better, but at the next table there was a bloke not much older than Steve, small gold earring, dressed in faded red leathers, who was reading a computer magazine. He went and sat there, stuffing the haversack under his chair.

Seconds later Red Leathers' meal arrived. As he put his magazine away in the courier bag hanging on the back of his chair, Steve tapped him on the shoulder.

" 'Scuse me, but have you got an *A–Z* I could borrow for a minute or two?"

"Sure," came the smiling reply. "You lost?"

"Sort of," Steve smiled back, taking the proffered, extremely dog-eared book. He'd opened it and was about to start looking at the detailed page when he realized that he needed to use it in conjunction with the tracker. In the middle of the café? He didn't think so. That would certainly raise a few eyebrows – he didn't look the type to be using that sort of high technology.

He was given no time to think what to do next as a greasy paper bag was thrust at him, followed by a demand for 75p. The waitress, sixty years old if she was a day, made change from the pound coin Steve gave her and was gone.

"Service isn't The Ritz, but the food's OK."

Steve looked up and saw it was Red Leathers talking to him; he also noticed the young man had nearly cleaned his plate already. "You look almost ready to go," he said. "I'd better give your book back . . ."

" 'SOK, I bought a new one yesterday," he said, wiping his plate with a slice of bread. "I was going to chuck it anyway – you can keep it if you want."

"You sure?"

"Course," he said, pushing his chair back and picking up his bag. "Hope you find where you're going."

Steve watched him go and pay, waving slightly as he left. You got the most unexpected kindness from the unlikeliest people, he thought, as the café's door closed behind him.

"Can we go now?" said Dachron.

"Are they a tribe, or what?" asked Dachron.

"Who?"

"The people in that place."

"The bikers?" said Steve, sitting down on a low wall. "No, not really a *tribe*, not even a gang. Some of them just like to look that way."

"All that metal on their faces," said Dachron, "the markings on their skin . . ."

"Yeah, I know." Steve began trying to match the outline schematic on the tracking unit to the complex map in the *A–Z*. "Scary, huh?"

Finding what he was looking for was a much tougher job than he'd hoped it would be, and Dachron wasn't much of a help as he was completely unused to reading

105

printed pages – especially when they were as worn and filthy as the ones in the book Steve had been given.

But finally Steve thought he'd worked out the actual location of where the tiny flashing light – the car they'd been following – had come to rest. It hadn't moved, and, hopefully, that meant Simon Tellkind was still somewhere nearby.

"Let's check it out," said Dachron. "I'm on a schedule here!"

"I know, I know!" said Steve, getting on the bike and powering up the drive. "I'm doing the best I can!" Indicating with his hand and pulling away from the pavement into the light traffic, he rode into what he'd heard called a "light industrial" district: faceless new factory units, glass and steel offices. Not a place with a huge amount of character, it occurred to Steve, a thought echoed by Dachron.

"This place get bombed and they rebuild from scratch?" he asked, as Steve turned down a road he reckoned would take him past where the car had stopped. The beeping from the tracking unit had been getting steadily faster, and now, the further down the street he went, the more hysterical it got.

"I think we're there," said Steve. "Either that or my pocket's about to explode."

Up ahead, sticking out from the side of a building, he could see a sign. As he got nearer he saw it belonged to an estate agent and read *Corporate HQ – Acquired for FPC by Tumbril Associates.*

"We're there," said Dachron. "Ride past it, see if we

can check out the sides and the back of the place – get a handle on what we're dealing with here."

"Can I turn the tracker off now?" asked Steve. "It's driving me crazy!"

"For now," said Dachron.

Steve glided by the building, seeing his reflection in the slate-grey mirrored glass of the huge front doors. He looked a mess, but then he hadn't had a shower for two days and had been sleeping rough on top of that. There was a left-hand turning at the end of the building and he took it, riding down a street one whole side of which was made up of the blank, windowless wall of the FPC headquarters.

He went left again and saw that the back of the building had set into it a large, factory-style metal door, the sort that's powered up and down by a motor. The doors were open as Steve cycled by, but the interior was dark and he couldn't make out anything that was going on. It wasn't the same for people inside.

Steve had just gone by the door, making for the end of the street and another left-hander that would take him back to where he'd started, when he heard someone shouting. He looked over his shoulder and saw a man come running out of the open gate, pointing and yelling, "It's him!"

It took a couple of precious seconds for the penny to drop and then Steve clicked that his own personal bucket of trouble was about to overflow.

"Grief . . ." he grunted, twisting the handlebar grip and hanging on like grim death as the power surge flung the bike forward.

"My feelings entirely," said Dachron. "Get us *outta* here!"

Behind him Steve could hear the echoing howl of an engine revving, then the high-pitched squeal as a clutch was dropped and rubber spun for traction on tarmac. They were coming after him.

Instead of going left as he'd intended, Steve hung a vicious right and took off down the street like a hare. He had no idea where he was going and for a moment couldn't care less, he just wanted to get away. Anywhere. The fact that there wasn't much traffic worked in his favour but also, he realized, in his pursuers'; he had to do something *they* couldn't do. As he shot round a gently curving crescent he saw a possibility – a road with bollards across it, leading to another street.

Steve accelerated, the bike leapt up on to the pavement and he steered it through the narrow gap. He *really* wanted to stop and give two fingers to the guys in the car he could now hear braking behind him, but he thought better of it and didn't even glance behind him as he tore off.

"Where to now?" said Steve, desperately searching for some landmark he recognized, something to make for.

"You're asking *me* – like *I* know where we are?"

"Dumb question . . ." Steve jumped a red light and heard an angry horn blast. If he didn't watch it he'd have the police after him as well. He'd been working on the principle that the people chasing him knew as little about where they were as he did, but he was wrong. As he sped down a nondescript road, concentrating on what was in front of him, he failed to notice the car coming up from behind.

Overtaking, it suddenly steered to the left, forcing him over into the gutter. Then Steve saw the flare of its brake lights and knew he was in trouble. He grabbed both levers on the handlebars, knowing there was no way he was going to stop himself crashing into the back of the car, but hit a major pothole instead.

"Jeeez . . ." he yelled as the bike's front wheel reared up. The jolt caused him to let go of the brakes and the back wheel, still on full power, spun him straight off the road and he virtually flew sideways into some bushes the other side of the pavement.

"Leave the bike and run!" Dachron's voice hissed inside Steve's head.

"Run?" mumbled Steve, picking himself up in time to see the car screech to a halt and two passenger doors come flinging open. "OK, run!"

One look at the twisted front wheel of the bike told him it wasn't going anywhere. There was nothing else to do but leg it, and as he took off in the opposite direction, the loosely-slung haversack slamming into him as he went, Steve knew in his heart of hearts that it was all over.

He was as good as caught; the footsteps behind him were getting closer, he could hear the whine of the car reversing back up the road and right now the streets were deserted. Twenty metres in front of him there was a T-junction – if he could make that, maybe, just *maybe* there would be some people about who would help him.

With one last burst of energy he picked up a little more

speed; Dachron's voice, forced to the back of his mind by the sheer panic and effort of what he was doing, was urging him on, on, on! Up ahead he saw a motorbike crossing his field of vision, from left to right, some part of his brain registering that the rider was wearing faded red leathers. Then he saw the rider swing across the road in a tight U-turn, waving.

"It's that guy who gave you the map!" yelled Dachron.

That was when Steve tripped on a paving-stone and, for the first time since he'd left primary school, did a flying somersault. He was travelling so fast, his haversack cushioning the impact on his back, that he rolled straight round and on to his feet again. Almost before he knew what he'd done he found himself skidding to a halt by the bike and its helmeted rider.

"You OK?" he asked, flipping his visor up.

"No!" Steve panted. "Those men . . ." He jerked a thumb over his shoulder. "They're trying to get me!"

"Jump on the back!" said the rider, dropping the visor. "And hold on tight!"

Steve didn't wait to be asked twice . . .

17

As the bike roared off down the road Steve stole a peek over his shoulder. The two men chasing him were back in their car, which was burning rubber as the driver attempted a record-breaking three-point turn. They weren't out of trouble by a long chalk.

Red Leathers was quite something, smoothly shifting through the gears as he wove the bike through the traffic on a fast, scary ride that Steve was glad he couldn't actually see. Hidden behind the man's back, holding on for dear life, the world whipped by him, a mad blur of colour and sound.

Leaning with the rider as he took a corner, Steve saw the car chasing them was now way behind and caught up in the building afternoon traffic.

"We're losing them!" he said, his words torn away by the wind.

"We might be," said Dachron, "but it ain't over till it's over – though I gotta say, I thought we'd had it before this guy turned up."

Steve was about to say something when he felt the bike slow down; the rider flipped his visor and shouted back: "Keep your head down – it's not too far now, but you're not wearing a helmet and I don't want to get pulled up by the cops!"

"OK!" Steve yelled back. Behind him he could hear the discordant blast of half a dozen people hitting their horns at the same time; craning his neck he saw the car chasing them was coming up the outside of the traffic – right over in the oncoming lane!

"These guys don't give up," muttered Dachron.

Steve didn't have a chance to answer. The rider had also seen what was happening in his rear-view mirror, the bike suddenly hauling away and then, just as suddenly ducking into a space between two cars and hanging a tight left turn. He could hear the clunk of the gear box and the whine of the engine as it slowed and then speeded up once more as the bike was flung hard right and off again.

It was like being on some wild roller-coaster ride – exhilarating, stomach-churning, too-fast-to-mention teeth-grinding . . . *magnificently* frightening; a huge, absurd paradox. Steve could feel his heart beating, was gasping for breath . . . almost hyperventilating . . . and so tense his muscles were beginning to scream. Going fast on the bicycle, with its charm-drive, was one thing, but this . . . this had noise, drama and the smell of grease, exhaust and oil. Every sense was under assault.

"Impressive," Steve heard Dachron say. "Technology's crap, but *he's* some pilot . . ."

This was, thought Steve, going to be very much a one-sided conversation – right now he couldn't reply because his jaw was clenched tight shut, and when – if – they got away with this he didn't know whether he'd want to relive it again.

Then he felt the bike slowing, not for another of those

asphalt-kissing turns, but slowing for a stop. Steve heard the light squeal of callipers biting on the front disc and then Red Leathers kicked the side stand and jumped off, leaving him sitting on the pillion seat, looking at a little dead-end street the sign up on the side of a house said was called Gibson Close. The bike was still running.

"What's he doing?" asked Dachron.

"Looks like he's opening some gates," whispered Steve, watching the man undo a padlock and swing back a pair of tall wooden gates to reveal an untidy concrete yard. Running back, he got back on the bike, dropped it into gear and rode it through the gates.

"Sorted! Off the road and out of sight," he said, going to pull the gates together and re-padlocking them from the inside. Turning round he took his helmet off, shaking his head to loosen his hair. "My name's Tony, by the way." He grinned and put out his hand.

"Right." Steve got off the bike, walked over and shook his hand. "I'm Steve, and . . . uh, thanks for getting me out of that."

Tony strolled back to the bike, opened its back box and took out the folded courier bag Steve had seen in the café. "Come on in, Steve. You look like you could do with a cup of coffee."

"You live here?"

"Yeah, upstairs," said Tony, choosing a key from the bunch he was holding. "This place belongs to one of my uncles; he's letting me use the top floor flat."

"Ask him if he can be traced here," said Dachron, "through that code number on the back of the machine, maybe? 'Cos if they can find us we better take off now."

"Is it safe?" asked Steve, hanging back.

"Safe?"

"Those men in the car – will they be able to find us here?"

"They the police or something?" said Tony, turning to look quizzically at Steve as he unlocked the back door. "What kind of trouble are you in?"

"They're not the police . . ." Steve could feel himself shaking, the adrenalin that had kept him going since he'd been spotted draining away fast. "And I've got no idea how big the trouble I'm in is."

"Take it easy," said Dachron, his voice low and calm. "You're doing fine. Just ask him about the bike."

"OK, come on . . . we'll—" Tony began to say.

"*Could* they trace your bike back here?" interrupted Steve, his voice rising. "Please, it's *very* important!"

Tony frowned and looked back at the red Honda CX 500 behind Steve. "It's registered at home, up in Edgware," he said, "and anyway, the plate's so filthy I doubt they could've made out the number . . . so, no, I don't think they can find out where we are."

"Fine . . . sorry . . . I didn't mean to shout."

"No problem," said Tony. "Come on up and tell me what this is all about."

Tony – Antoni Michaelides, as it turned out – was a nineteen-year-old student studying computer science at the Imperial College. In the holidays he did motorcycle messengering to help supplement his grant. He lived in the tiny one-bedroom flat because, he said, *anything* was better than living at home with a mum who still treated him as if he was thirteen and a dad who thought he should spend *all* his time studying for his exams.

Apart from its one bedroom, the flat had a tiny kitchen, an even tinier bathroom and a sitting-room stuffed with books, magazines, CDs and computer equipment. Every flat surface had things piled on it, including the floor.

"Heaven!" said Steve when he saw it. "No one to make you tidy up."

"Too right," said Tony, coming out of the kitchen with two mugs of instant coffee and handing one to Steve. "So . . . what's this all about? Why were those guys after you?"

Steve moved a pile of motorbike magazines off the threadbare sofa and sat down with a sigh. "It's a long story, Tony," he said, blowing on the dark brown liquid in the Tottenham Hotspur mug.

"I'm not planning on going anywhere."

"Don't tell him everything," said Dachron. "He doesn't need to know, and he'd never believe you anyway."

Steve spread his hands out, palms up, in front of him and shrugged silently, hoping Dachron would get the message to tell him just exactly what *to* say. He did.

"Tell him this is about your father," said Dachron. "Say he's involved in some kind of business deal – you don't know what – and those men were trying to get you to make your father do what they want . . . OK?"

Steve nodded to himself and looked over at an expectant

Tony. "It's my dad," he said slowly, trying to sound like he was telling the truth. "Some business deal of his . . ."

"What's he do?"

"He's a pr . . . he's a scientist," Steve corrected himself quickly. "Some people he's involved with are trying to get at him through me."

"Why don't you go to the cops?"

"Too dangerous," prompted Dachron.

"Too dangerous," repeated Steve.

"Who *are* these people?" asked Tony, swinging round the swivel chair in front of his computer and sitting down on it.

"Future Power," Steve blurted out before he could stop himself.

"Damn!" said Dachron. "Shouldn't've told him that!"

Too late now, thought Steve.

"Future Power? Never heard of them," Tony shook his head. "What're you going to do?"

"Dunno."

"Stay here as long as you want," offered Tony, "but you'll have to leave *eventually*."

"I know." Steve leaned back; he was tired, worn out by the constant chasing, him chasing them, them chasing him – and he must have looked it.

"You can crash out any time you like," said Tony. "Have my bed. I'm planning on working through tonight anyway. Gotta catch up with my project work. We'll talk in the morning."

"Thanks . . . you sure?"

"Sure I'm sure." Tony smiled, looking at his watch.

"Look, it's nearly 5 o'clock. I'm going to cook something for supper – house speciality: pasta, just like Mama makes."

"I thought you were Greek?" said Steve.

"Greek mums call it *macaronia du furnu*, but it's the same kinda thing."

"You cook?"

"When your parents own a restaurant," Tony said, getting up, "you cook."

The meal was great, tasty and filling, the can of beer Steve had with it cold and welcome, and Tony, true to his word, hadn't said a thing about what had happened. The combination of food, drink and the day's events made Steve slow down and feel even more tired; his eyes were gritty, his limbs heavy and all he wanted to do was lie down. For ever.

Tony told him to forget helping with the dishes and to get himself off to bed, and Steve was in no condition to argue. He went like a lamb, collapsing on top of Tony's duvet and crashing out almost immediately. He had no recollection at all of the blanket being laid over him.

Leaving the bedroom door half open, Tony took their plates into the kitchen and put them in the sink to soak, along with the last two days' washing-up. That would all get done when there were no more clean plates left.

He went back and switched on his computer and external modem. Once all his software had loaded up he logged on to his net server and jumped into the Web. The keyboard clicked furiously and the mouse in his right hand made the cursor fly over the flowing screen in front of him as he picked his way from site to site, searching.

"Future Power," he murmured to himself. "If they're as big as he's making out, they'll be here somewhere . . ."

18

Day 4 – Wednesday, 4th April 2007. 12.35 a.m.

The digital clock on top of the monitor flashed the time – well after midnight. Tony was still hunched over his keyboard and beside him was a pad covered with scrawled notes. He'd spent hours trawling through databases all over the shop, following the tangled mesh of interlacing strands of information that, so far, had produced no hard facts whatsoever about the Future Power Corporation – as he now knew was its full name.

He'd been bitten by the need-to-know bug, and all thoughts of his project work had been pushed well to one side. It could wait. Tony felt like some kind of post-modern investigator, a cyber-tec prowling the ether for clues; as that particular thought meandered across his brain he realized he'd probably had enough coffee, and could well do with taking at least half an hour's rest before he carried on poking about in various dusty corners of the net.

Leaning back in his chair he stretched his arms behind him, hearing the soft, satisfying *pop!* of his muscles de-crunching. "Maybe a cup of tea," he said out loud, swinging his chair round.

Standing in the bedroom door he saw a silhouetted figure looking at him and for a second his heart leapt and he jerked backwards. Then he remembered his guest. It wasn't a burglar or a homicidal prowler, just Steve.

"You awake?" said Tony. "I was just going to make a cup of tea – want one?"

Steve didn't say anything for a moment and in the midnight silence Tony could hear an odd *KLIK-KLIK-KLIKETY-KLIK* sound. At first he thought it might be his printer malfunctioning, and then he realized it was Steve nervously snapping his fingers.

"Steve?" Tony got up. "You OK?"

"Yeah . . . yeah, I'm fine," said Dachron. This was the third time he'd taken over Steve's body, had complete control of the flesh and bones he now shared, and each time it was a fight. The other side, Steve's persona, didn't like giving up its dominance; reaching out was like forcing himself through to the head of a tightly-packed crowd; he had to push in front of the prime mind, and the prime mind sub-consciously hated the intruder and didn't want him there.

"Tea?"

"No thanks," said Dachron, shaking his head and rubbing sleep from his eyes. It had taken him some time to take enough control to get out of bed and walk to the door, but now he felt OK, in charge of this strange body. Now he had a job to do; once again he couldn't afford to wait until Steve woke up to do things. He watched Tony go into the kitchen and went over to Steve's jacket and checked the tracker. The car hadn't moved.

This next bit was going to be tricky. He had to convince the young man to take him back to the FPC building, right now. He *had* to get in there and locate Simon Tellkind before they moved him – because, now the bike was trashed, he'd have no way of following them if they decided to go elsewhere. It was tonight or he'd probably never get this close again.

Although it was only Wednesday, and he still had four days left, all his training and years of field experience had taught him that if the target was in sight, shoot. Trust that your skills would enable you to hit it, because the chances were you'd never have another chance.

Tony came back in with a cup in one hand and a packet of biscuits in the other. "Want one?" he asked, holding the packet out. "They're bourbons."

Dachron shook his head. "No thanks, not hungry . . . Look, Tony, I need a favour."

"What?"

"I need you to take me back near to where you picked us – *me* – up. There's something I've got to do."

"Tomorrow," said Tony, stuffing half a biscuit in his mouth, "you want to go back tomorrow and see if you can get your bike, right?"

"No, I want to go *now*!"

"Now?" Tony glanced at his watch. "It's 12.30!"

KLIK-KLIK-KLIKETY-KLIK.

"I can't explain *why* I need to go, Tony." Dachron could feel himself tensing. He wasn't used to asking, he gave orders and things happened. "The situation I'm in, it's *very* complicated . . . dangerous and complicated. I haven't got the time to go into details, and I doubt whether you'd believe me if I told you *any* of what's going down . . ."

"Try me." Tony sat down by his computer, its screen covered in flying toasters.

"No."

"Eh?"

"The less you know, the better."

Tony stared at Dachron, frowning slightly, puzzled at the change in the way Steve was acting. The young boy had a much harder edge to him, more *adult*, somehow, and there was something in his eyes, the way he held himself, the constant nervy finger-clicking . . . it was almost as if he was a different person.

"You're tired, I'm tired, I've got work to do and it's late," he said. "Go back to bed and we'll do whatever it is you want in the morning. OK?"

Dachron wanted to grab Tony by the throat and make him understand, in a very *physical* way, that this was more in the way of a command than a request. Somehow he managed to damp down the fire, close the door on his anger; he had a strong feeling that the young man in front of him would react better to reason than violence.

It occurred to him that he'd been trying to get through to Tony in his own way, but how would a sixteen-year-old go about it? An exhausted, emotional sixteen-year-old whose father was in deep trouble? Dachron's mind raced as he stared straight back at Tony . . . and then he burst into tears.

Tony looked at the boy standing in front of him, all the bravado and front he'd been showing since he'd woken up disappearing as he sobbed his heart out. He felt really sorry for him and got up. "It's OK, Steve," he said, putting a hand on his shoulder. "Let's talk about this . . . see what we can do . . ."

It was cold on the back of the bike. Tony had lent Steve a black jersey, which he was wearing under his denim jacket, but he was still shivering. "Breaking down" had done the trick, and Tony had agreed to take him out to Docklands; Dachron had let him carry on thinking it was to look for his bicycle and the two of them were cruising around looking for the street where he'd crashed.

"It's that turning on the left," said Tony, slowing down.

"Drop me here," said Dachron, reaching up to his chin to undo the helmet Tony had made him wear. He was going to have to lose the boy and find his own way over to the FPC building – a trick that might be more difficult than getting out of the house in the first place.

"Drop you?" said Tony, pulling up.

Dachron jumped off the pillion seat and handed the helmet over. "Yeah, I need to look around here by myself for a bit."

"At *this* time of night?" Tony frowned. "What the hell's going on, Steve? I can't leave you out here, wandering round on your own – it's nearly three o'clock!"

Dachron stood looking at Tony. He could feel his fingers itching to click and knew he had to tell the kid something, slowly realizing that he could actually be of some use. He took a deep breath. "There are reasons I can't tell you everything, Tony," he said, "and there's no reason at all why you should help me any more than you already have." He paused, still not sure he should take the risk.

"But?"

"But I've got to have a look at a building round here and I can only do it on my own."

KLIK-KLIK-KLIKETY-KLIK.

Dachron's fingers got the better of him and he gave up trying to stop them. "Give me your phone number, and if I haven't called you in a couple of hours, get in touch with someone – the police, whoever – and tell them where I am."

"Where will that be?" asked Tony.

"The Future Power Corporation."

"They're here?"

"Not far," said Dachron. "I think my father's in there . . ."

"This is stupid!" said Tony. "It's a crazy plan . . . not a *plan* at all! What am I doing even listening to you? Get back on the bike and let's go home."

Tony angrily threw the helmet back at Dachron and he caught it like a football, slightly taken aback by the response. This whole situation was beyond anything he'd ever had to deal with – here he was, trapped in partial command of a body so far out of his own time that it was beyond imagining, and unable to exercise any real control over events. A lesser person might've gone mad, but he knew he'd been chosen for this insane mission precisely because he was a man who could operate under pressure. He carefully handed the helmet back to Tony.

"My name is Dachron Amok," he said, looking Tony straight in the eye. "I am a Line Sergeant in an elite anti-terrorist squad of the United Southern States Army. I have been sent back – via a process I am told is called

Temporal Ribbon Placement – from the year 2667 to find a man called Simon Tellkind. That I do so is of paramount importance, and I can allow *nothing* to get in my way. My belief is that the man I want is being held inside the Future Power building. OK?"

"Steve?" said Tony, switching off the bike and taking his own helmet off. "What the *hell* are you talking about?"

"Steve is asleep," said Dachron. "Hard to believe as it may seem, because of what I'm sure the guys who invented the damned process would call 'an irregularity', we are sharing the same body . . . I only get to do my thing when he crashes out."

"Stone me!" said Tony.

" 'Scuse me?"

"Whatever . . . you're joking, right?"

"No."

"I'm outta here, OK?" said Tony, reaching round and putting Dachron's helmet in the back box. "You are *really* pissing me off – I'm going home."

"Good," said Dachron. "You go home, you do your work – and if I don't call you by five o'clock, like I said, do what I asked."

"Sure."

"Contact number?" asked Dachron.

Tony took a biro and crumpled pad out of a pocket and wrote something down. Tearing the sheet off he handed it to Dachron.

"Thanks," he said. "See you later, Tony."

Tony rammed his helmet back on and fired up the bike. "Whatever," he said, and rode away.

19

Day 4 – Wednesday, 4th April 2007. 3.30 a.m.

Whoever had designed the FPC building had done a good job on security. There were only two ways in at ground level – the mirror-glassed front entrance or the steel-gated rear. It was a cloudy night, no moon, and Dachron had spent quite some time scouting round, flitting from shadow to shadow, checking out the whole place.

Motor-driven closed-circuit TV cameras, with infrared lights, hugged each corner and bright halogen spots washed the front and rear entrances with their harsh, cold light. From what Dachron could make out from his observations the cameras only moved if something happened on the street, otherwise they stayed put in a position that he assumed someone had thought gave the best possible view all round the building.

"Lazy," he said to himself as he figured out that there were "dead" areas where, when the cameras were at rest, nothing could be seen. "Lazy and sloppy."

Crouched in a doorway across the street, Dachron began to put things together. Down the right-hand side of the building he could see a line of windows – one of which was partially open – giving on to what must be the first floor. A wide sill ran along underneath them, which was too high off the ground to reach from the pavement, but if someone climbed up one of the metal lampposts in the "dead" area and jumped . . .

From what Dachron had already seen of the FPC security arrangements there was more than a fair chance that no one would've thought to alarm the windows – and a fair chance was about as good as he was going to get. All he had to do was wait for a car to drive down the street and he'd be off and running.

As he sat on his heels in the cold, damp doorway he wondered whether Tony would do as he'd asked. If he'd read him right, and he'd always thought of himself as a good judge of character, Tony still believed he was a sixteen-year-old boy – possibly one who'd gone a little crazy in the head, but still sixteen. That being the case, if he got into trouble and didn't phone him Tony'd probably make the call – which might be the only lifeline he'd have. He was going into this place unarmed, his only weapons being his wit, hands and feet. A worry, but what else could he do?

In the back of his mind Dachron felt Steve's slumbering self rise up close to the surface; it was weird, like having a growth somewhere you couldn't reach – annoying, but somehow you got used to it. Handleable, as long as he didn't wake up. And then he heard the car.

It came down the street at a leisurely pace, the driver obviously in no kind of hurry. Dachron moved to the edge of the doorway and watched the dark saloon come towards him, its dipped headlights casting moving shadows along the pavement. He could see the camera on the nearest corner jerk slightly as it picked up the movement and automatically start to follow the car.

Using the car as cover, Dachron hurried across the pavement to hide behind a pile of black rubbish bags that had been put out for collection in the morning. Eyes locked on the camera he watched it pan round and keep on tracking the saloon; any moment now it would reach the limit of its turn and would begin to swing back. This was it – there would, he calculated, be about ten seconds in which he could run across the street and make it to the lamppost he reckoned was in the dead area.

Dachron was off the blocks like an Olympic sprinter, powering over the road. If anyone happened to look out of a window now he was lost, but he dismissed the thought and concentrated on getting to the relative safety of the tall metal post.

No sirens had gone off, no one had come running out on to the street and, as far as he could tell, he hadn't set off any other alarms climbing through the half-open window. Even jumping across the gap between the lamppost and the sill hadn't been *that* difficult, although he was becoming aware of the limitations of being in Steve's body.

"Fit you ain't," muttered Dachron as he made off down a low-lighted corridor.

Somewhere in this building was the man with the future of the world in his head, and, if luck was with him, he was near to finding him and completing his job. Sounded too good to be true, thought Dachron, who knew from bitter experience how easy it was for things to go wrong at the last moment.

In this situation, under normal circumstances, he'd be

in peak physical condition and psyched-up to the max. Tight, like a wire. But here he was, a grown man – a trained killer no less – tracking down some scientist while he was trapped in the body of a sixteen-year-old boy, a body he still shared with that boy. Part of Dachron's military training had been having the notion bludgeoned into him that the job got done *whatever the circumstances*. He shook his head – no one could ever have been trained for circumstances like these.

Now, using all the skill he could muster, he had to discover the whereabouts of Simon Tellkind and persuade him to change his stupid charm-drive formula, and what he needed was some information. The quickest way to get it, in his experience, was to make someone give it to you, whether they wanted to or not. What he wanted to find was someone on their own.

But the building seemed to be eerily deserted. He'd gone up and down almost every corridor on the first floor, checked every unlocked room, and come across no one. It was almost as if he'd gone to all that trouble to break into an empty building. Dachron was just about to go looking on the next floor when he smelt something acrid in the air: cigarette smoke.

He stopped and listened. Not far away he could hear the sound of music playing and as he crept down the carpeted passageway it got louder and the smell of the smoke stronger. He stopped outside a partially open office door and psyched himself up, taking deep breaths and clearing his mind of all other distractions. And then he opened the door and walked in.

"Who the hell are you?" said the startled man sitting at a desk in the windowless room.

Dachron didn't say anything. He closed the door behind him and walked across the room. His fingers snapped, *KLIK-KLIK-KLICKETY-KLIK*, as he made his way towards the man.

"What are you doing here, kid?" demanded the man, stubbing his cigarette out as he stood up.

Dachron walked round the desk and punched him in the stomach. Not hard, but hard enough to wind him. "Shut up," he whispered in the man's ear as he folded, "and listen . . ."

The whole thing hadn't taken more than five minutes, tops. Tied to his chair and threatened with his own silenced pistol the man had spilled everything he knew as if Dachron had pressed his PLAY button. The fact that it looked like a young boy was doing all this to him had helped considerably. Simon Tellkind, he now knew, was in a room on the floor above, towards the front of the building. At least one guard, possibly two.

Leaving the man gagged and trussed to his chair, Dachron had locked the room and made his way upstairs. Now he had a gun he felt much less vulnerable, but he didn't let that stop him from being ultra-cautious – no point in tempting Fate if you didn't have to, especially now he was so close. Rule No. 1 in the *Survival Handbook*.

At the top of the darkened stairwell it became obvious that the second floor was where all the activity was taking place in the building. It could be more difficult getting around up here. Dachron stood in the shadows and watched through the small wire-reinforced window set in the door and in his mind's eye he constructed a floor plan, trying to work out the quickest route to the room where Tellkind was.

It was almost like meditating, at least until the calm state he'd put himself in was rudely jarred by Steve. Something had disturbed his sleep pattern and a wave of distorted mental images flooded over Dachron, making him grab hold of the steel banisters, the cold metal feeling almost damp to the touch.

"Go away!" Dachron hissed through gritted teeth. "Stay outta this, Steve!"

Centring himself, pushing Steve's dulled presence aside, Dachron fought to regain control . . . and finally won. He shook his head; the last thing he needed now was for Steve to wake up and freak out.

Waiting until he couldn't hear anyone on the other side of the door, Dachron pushed down on the smooth aluminium handle and pulled the door towards him. Sneaking out he let the door snick shut behind him and stood for a second or two, getting himself oriented and listening. With the heavy weight of the gun in his hand, its barrel double its normal length because of the silencer, he moved off in the direction the man had told him to go.

He walked quickly, almost in a trance state. This had to be done fast, no time for second thoughts, no time to wonder if what he was doing was right or not – any mistakes would have to be dealt with as and when they happened. In any kind of action, this was the only way. Trust your instincts and be so quick that your enemy has no time to react.

Turning a corner he spotted a man lounging in a chair outside a room, some five metres away. As the man caught sight of him, Dachron saw him reach inside his jacket and caught a look of total incomprehension in his eyes. It was still there after he'd shot him.

Without even glancing over his shoulder Dachron ran up to the slumped body and checked what he'd been reaching for. It wasn't his wallet. Turning the door handle he found it wasn't locked; opening it he switched the light on. He'd made it.

"Time to wake up, Mr Tellkind," he said to the man lying fully clothed and with one wrist handcuffed to the metal-framed bed. "I've got something to tell you . . ."

20

Day 4 – Wednesday, 4th April 2007. 4.15 a.m.

Dachron's mind was in hyper-drive. Adrenalin flooded his system and he could feel the spike as the tiny gland near his kidneys released its powerful hormone into his bloodstream. It felt good to be back at work. It felt even better knowing he was minutes from delivering his message and completing his task.

Hauling the dead man off his chair Dachron laid him on the floor inside the room, flicked the internal lock on the door and turned to look at Tellkind. He'd got his glasses off the table by the bed and was now sitting up and staring at him.

"Who on *earth* are you?" he said, his eyes flicking nervously from gun to the body on the floor. "What's going on?"

"You don't recognize me?" asked Dachron, smiling.

"No . . ."

"I'm Richard Anthony's boy, Steve," said Dachron. "Well, mostly."

"What are *you* doing here at" – Tellkind looked at his watch – "a quarter past four in the morning, Steven?"

"Long story, Mr Tellkind, and no time to tell it." Dachron walked over to the bed, put the muzzle of the gun on the handcuffs and shot the lock out; freeing the man might make him more prepared to listen. "We've got other things to talk about before someone realizes your guard has gone AWOL."

"Is he . . . dead?" asked Tellkind, frowning; too shocked by the speed at which events were happening, he seemed not to realize he was now at liberty to stand up.

Dachron glanced at the body on the floor. "Who cares?" he said.

"This is unbelievable! What are you doing here . . . with a *gun*?" spluttered Tellkind. "Does your father know where you are?"

"My father hasn't even been born yet." Dachron pulled up a chair and sat down. "Now listen carefully, because I don't think I'm going to have a chance to say this twice: you have invented something called the Charm Principle, and I am here to tell you that there is a fatal flaw in your calculations."

Simon Tellkind's face froze, and then his right eyelid began to twitch. "Who *are* you?" he said, very quietly. "I only named it the Charm Principle three days ago . . . and I haven't told anyone, not a single person."

"Listen to me." Dachron snapped his fingers in front of Tellkind's face to get his attention. "In the secondary subloop of the Principle's data stream there is an anomaly . . ." Dachron's voice flattened out as he spoke the words he'd been coached to memorize by heart; he had no idea what they meant. "If the prime algorithm is left in place the end result is the production of subatomic exhaust particles, which causes something called the Scattering Effect. This randomly unglues atomic structures and eventually destroys everything. If the prime algorithm is altered, adding the recursive element E minus O equals the square root of T, the outcome will be heuristic, in the pure sense."

Tellkind's jaw had dropped and he was blinking hard.

"Did you understand all that?" asked Dachron. "Did it make sense?"

"Yes."

"Good. Now, whatever you do, don't forget a world I just said." Dachron got up. He couldn't help smiling – he'd done it, and with a couple of days to spare. "I have to go now, before anyone finds me."

"You can't just *leave*, Steven!" said Tellkind, leaping off the bed and grabbing Dachron's arm, the shattered handcuff swinging like some strange piece of jewellery. "What's going on around here? The last few days have been a nightmare; everything's gone completely crazy!"

Dachron had no trouble believing that – Sunday afternoon was when he and Steve had set the cat among the pigeons by starting to look for Simon Tellkind. No wonder the man had had a hard time since then; whoever he was *really* working for (and, from what Dachron could make out, there had to be some dark people behind Future Power) had potent reasons for not wanting him found.

"Steven?" said Tellkind. "Are you listening to me? Is your father involved in this – does he know why I'm being treated like this . . . like a common criminal?"

Dachron focused back on Tellkind. "I'm not Steven Anthony," he said.

"Then who the hell *are* you?"

"I come from the future, Mr Tellkind, over six hundred years in the future." Dachron shook Tellkind's hand off his arm. "And if you don't do what I just told you that's as far as the future's gonna get."

"Not Steven . . . ?" A look of complete confusion swept Tellkind's face. "What do you mean . . . how? You can't just leave now . . . I know my work's important, but—"

"You wouldn't believe me if I told you any more, Mr Tellkind," said Dachron. "I hardly credit it myself. But the future I come from depends on your work in ways you couldn't understand."

"And this mistake, this anomaly, is so important?"

"Making those changes is going to be the most important thing you'll *ever* do," said Dachron, looking directly into Tellkind's eyes. "Six hundred years from now they'll still be talking about you . . . and there have been precious few people in history who that's ever happened to, Mr Tellkind."

A noise outside the room made Dachron switch back from messenger into soldier. As he swung round the door burst open, the area round the lock splintering; all he saw were the barrels of the two guns pointing at him.

His first thought was to empty the clip in the gun and be done with it, but a millisecond later he realized that if there was a fire fight Tellkind could just as easily get hit as him. And that would be entirely counterproductive. Dachron dropped the pistol and put both hands up in the air.

The men stormed into the room. One of them he recognized as the man who'd opened the door to the house in Berkhamsted and been in on the chase through Docklands.

"It's that bloody kid again!" he said, grabbing one of Dachron's arms and viciously twisting it behind him.

"Morton's dead, one shot back of his ear," said the other one, kneeling by the body on the floor. "A pro job, can't've been the kid . . . there must be someone else."

"He's got the gun," said the one holding Dachron, "but buzz Denner in the control room and get the place searched ASAP – and tell him we're probably going to have to move the schedule forward on getting Tellkind to Geneva. Mr Landorff's going to go ballistic when he finds out this has happened."

Dachron stood completely still. Behind him he could hear the bedsprings squeaking as Simon Tellkind sat back down on the mattress, but the scientist didn't say anything; he must be in shock, thought Dachron.

"How'd you get in – and where's the other guy?" The man jerked Dachron's arm even harder, sharp stabs of pain shooting up his neck from his tortured shoulder.

"Open window," said Dachron, grimacing; in the background he could hear the second man talking on a phone.

"And the *other* person?" the man hissed in Dachron's ear, wrenching his arm up even further.

"Nobody else," said Dachron; as he fought against the pain a groaning filled his head. For a moment he couldn't work out what it was, and then he realized that Steve was finally waking up . . .

21

Day 4 – Wednesday, 4th April 2007. 5.05 a.m.

Tony was worried. Not only had Steve – or whoever the hell the boy was he'd left in Docklands – not called him, but he'd found out enough about the Future Power Corporation to make the hairs on the back of his neck stand on end.

As soon as he'd got back home he'd logged back on to the net. Tony had been a hacker almost since he'd got his hands on his first computer; he'd never been caught, but a couple of times it had got very close. With all the practice he'd had over the years Tony was now very, very good at getting into places people thought were totally secure, but following the trail of FPC had been just about the toughest thing he'd ever done.

It had involved major excavations in mainframes and databases on three continents, with some fairly nifty code-breaking on his part using a decryption program he had on his laptop, but eventually he'd got enough information to make a picture. Pretty it was not.

As far as he could tell Future Power was ultimately owned by an obscure Russian organization, based in Moscow, but with influence in just about every financial centre on the globe. They were into currency, arms, pharmaceuticals and energy, and that was only the semi-legal stuff that was near the surface; given time Tony was sure there was a hell of a lot more to find out.

But right then, at five minutes past Steve's deadline for calling in, Tony didn't need to know any more to be certain that he was probably up to his neck and beyond in trouble. Quite what to do about it was another matter entirely. Steve had said to call the police, but Tony didn't think he'd have much luck there – who'd take any notice of his story at this time in the morning?

He'd shut down his computer and was sitting in front of the blank screen, staring at his fuzzy reflection. He had to do something; he couldn't just sit there in his flat and chew his nails. Whoever Steve was he couldn't simply abandon him to some people who'd make the Cosa Nostra look like a bunch of cissies, but what other options did he have?

Tony got up and went to the bathroom to have a pee. Then he made another cup of coffee and sat back down in front of the computer. Professor Horowitz was going to hang him out to dry for not getting his project finished . . . *Professor Horowitz!* Why hadn't he thought of him before? His course director was a man with some serious connections – he did consultancy work for a string of multinational companies and, rumour had it, more than a little of his personal funding came from government agencies. And Tony had his home phone number.

It was nearly 5.15, not a time you'd call most people up, but Jim Horowitz always boasted that he was one of Nature's early risers. "Let's see if you're telling the truth,"

Tony muttered to himself as he punched the number into his phone's keypad.

"Yes?" barked a voice so loud it made Tony jump.

"Prof?" said Tony. "It's Tony Michaelides. Have you got a minute? You're the only person I could think of who might be able to help . . ."

The rumours had been right. Less than half an hour after explaining things to the Professor two unmarked government-issue Vauxhalls had whispered to a halt outside his flat and Tony found himself going over everything again. This time it was to a group of sternfaced individuals who didn't seem to think it necessary to explain who they were, what they did or where they worked. He was beginning to think that maybe the police hadn't been such a bad idea after all.

There were six of them, but two had stayed with the cars, which was good, because there wasn't enough room for them in the flat. And this lot obviously hadn't read the bit in the manual where it said you had to show your ID and be pleasant to people.

"Right," said the one who'd introduced himself as Mr Harker. "Where did you say this boy came from?"

"I told you. I met him yesterday afternoon in a café near the courier office," said Tony.

"Tell me again."

"I gave him my old *A–Z* in the café," Tony went on," and then later on I saw him again, being chased by some guys."

"And you brought him back here."

"Yes." Tony was leaning against the kitchen sink, Mr Harker was blocking the doorway and behind him Tony could see the other three going through his notes and printouts about Future Power.

"You didn't think it odd, a car in hot pursuit of a young boy?" said Mr Harker. "Not worth reporting to the police?"

"He asked me not to, pleaded really," shrugged Tony. "Thought I'd sort it out in the morning."

"And then he asked you to take him back."

"Yeah, woke up about half past twelve and was very strange," said Tony, "like another person, almost."

"So you went back and left him there, on his own – why?"

"Like I said, he was a different person." Tony shook his head, remembering how violent and weird Steve had got. "Changed his mind about it being his father who he was looking for and told me it was someone else. Anyway, he made me promise to do something if he didn't contact me by five o'clock . . . and then I discovered all that stuff about Future Power and called the Prof."

"A good choice," said Mr Harker.

"Well, I doubt you lot are in the phone book," Tony grinned.

"This isn't funny, Mr Michaelides." Mr Harker rubbed his jaw; he looked harassed, like he had too many things to think about and not enough time for any of them. "The man's name, the one he said he had to find – are you sure you can't remember what it was?"

Tony had been racking his brains since the first time

he'd been asked. "Telcker . . . something like that?" he said.

"Tellkind?" said Mr Harker.

"Yeah! That's it – Tellkind! You heard of him?"

Mr Harker ignored Tony, turning to the men in the other room. "They've got Tellkind in there – must be getting ready to move him out of the country," he said. "Get hold of Duke and the second unit and have him meet me here, pronto!"

"Right, sir!" said one of the others, and as he reached into his jacket for his mobile phone Tony saw he was carrying a gun under his arm.

"What's going on?" he asked, but before he could get an answer Mr Harker was called by the two men looking at the printouts.

"Stay there," he said. "I'll be back in a moment."

A wave of tiredness swept over Tony; he hadn't slept for what seemed like days and everything ached. He turned on the cold tap in the sink and splashed handfuls of water on his face, the icy liquid clearing his head. He was drying himself off with a relatively clean tea-towel when Mr Harker came back.

"You're almost too clever for your own good, son," he said, stopping in the doorway again.

"Eh?"

"I hope you weren't careless about covering your tracks out there in cyberspace, Mr Michaelides."

"Why?"

"The people whose digital domain you were wandering around are not known for their reticence in dealing with those they consider troublemakers," said Mr Harker.

"I've not been caught before."

"So I gather."

Tony was about to ask what the bad guys would do to him if they found out who he was when he heard a soft knock on his front door.

"That'll be Duke. Let him in, will you?" Mr Harker said over his shoulder.

The man who walked in was wearing camouflage body armour and carrying what was clearly a high-powered rifle with a serious set of night sights. "Ready when you are," he said.

22

Day 4 – Wednesday, 4th April 2007. 5.15 a.m.

Steve was terrified. He was strapped to a chair in a room with no windows and there were two men shouting questions at him; he thought he recognized one of them but for the life of him couldn't remember where from. The last thing *he* remembered was going to bed at Tony's flat.

"Where's your friend?" yelled the man he vaguely recognized, his face so close to Steve's he could see the individual hairs on his chin and smell his sour breath.

"What friend? I don't know what you're talking about!" said Steve, turning his head away. He had a good idea how he'd got to this place, and where it was, but as he hadn't heard a word from Dachron since he'd woken up he didn't know the details.

"Come on, kid – where's the other guy?" The man grabbed Steve's face and pulled it back.

"I told you – I've no idea how I got here, and there *is* no other guy!" Steve said as calmly as he could, all the time wondering why they kept going on about there being someone else. What had Dachron done while he'd been in charge?

"Look —" the man stood back, took a cigarette out of a pack on a nearby table and lit it; he sucked the smoke in as if he'd just surfaced from a long dive – "if you don't tell the truth" – he exhaled all over Steve – "you'll be the one who takes the rap for the shooting."

"What . . . what shooting?" Steve could feel his heart pumping *BU-BABA-BU-BABA*. "I don't know anything about any shooting . . ."

The other man hit him, smacked his face with the flat of his hand. "Don't get clever, son," he sneered. "Getting clever would be a very stupid thing to do right now."

Steve's cheek stung from the slap. His mind was racing but it wasn't going anywhere – nothing made sense. For the first time since it had happened he wished Dacron was there in his head to tell him what to do, but, just when he needed him, he was being uncharacteristically silent. It occurred to Steve that his waking up in the middle of things might have something to do with it, but Dachron's sudden disappearance wasn't helping him figure out why these people thought he was supposed to have shot someone. The man with the cigarette leaned forward again and Steve suddenly remembered where he'd seen him before – opening the door to Simon Tellkind's house!

"Look, Steven," he said, holding his cigarette uncomfortably close to Steve's hand, "we know who you are, where you live . . . We just want to know who your friend is and why he's been bothering us."

"Let's cut the crap," said the man who'd slapped him, punching a number into the phone. "I'm getting the quack."

This was nothing like the good-guy, bad-guy interview

technique Steve had seen on all the TV cop shows he'd watched; this was bad-guy all the way. He was quite sure the two men giving him a hard time definitely weren't policemen. And it was guaranteed that the weasel-faced man who he saw coming into the room with a hypodermic needle in his hand wasn't a doctor . . .

Tony looked at his watch and in the dim light he saw it was ten to six; things were moving at an incredible pace. He was in the back of a Transit that was packed with all kinds of high-tech electronic surveillance equipment – not that he wanted to be. Nice Mr Harker had insisted he come along for the ride ("to help with identification," he'd said) but Tony had the very strong impression he was as good as under arrest.

From what he could make out from the rapid-fire conversations he'd heard, the whole area round the Future Power building had been cordoned off. Through the small bit of the windscreen visible from where he sat Tony had seen the occasional pedestrian and bloke on a bike, a postal van and a milk float pass by, the kind of traffic you'd expect for that time of the morning. Except none of the people out there were who they appeared to be.

Tony hadn't actually been told anything (except what to do), but he was a good listener and had put together a picture of what was going on, though admittedly a pretty sketchy one. Harker and his people just *had* to be government, with all the tech they'd got and the way they were riding roughshod over everybody. But it was the controlled panic brought on by the news of Simon

Tellkind's involvement that he couldn't work out. The man must be something really special.

"Sector reports," Mr Harker snapped into the hands-free mic that looped in front of his mouth. "All secure? Do we have all the phone lines monitored? OK, and what about their microwave link? Well, get the damn thing jammed then!"

Harker swung round in his seat and barked at the man next to him. "What's happening with the sound and vision?"

"Pictures and words coming in any minute now, sir."

"And about bloody time too!"

Whatever agency or department Harker worked for, they had access to some pretty swift equipment and an impressive amount of manpower. High-gain cameras, plus microphones that were so sensitive they could pick up conversations from the vibrations in the windows, were trained on the building, and as he watched he saw half a dozen small screens flicker into life with grainy black and white pictures.

"Is the chopper up?" asked Harker.

"Right overhead, sir."

"Why can't we hear it?" asked Tony, his curiosity getting the better of him.

"Because it's a stealth jobby, sunshine," replied Harker without even looking at him. "The Yanks lent it to us on the understanding we didn't bend it."

Tony sat back. Whoever Simon Tellkind was, he thought, the powers that be really didn't want Future Power to have him. With time on his hands, and no one taking any notice of him, he reran the last time he'd seen Steve; events made him think much harder about what was going on.

Something had happened to Steve between the time he'd crashed out and when he'd woken up, something so weird Tony hadn't dared tell Harker. What if it was true – what if he really was sharing his body with a man from the twenty-seventh century . . . ?

23

Day 4 – Wednesday, 4th April 2007. 5.46 a.m.

The needle went through his skin, sliding easily into his vein. Steve could do nothing but watch. One man was behind him, holding him by the neck and chest, the other had his arm clamped to the chair while the quack, as they'd called him, proceeded with the injection. And then they all stood back.

"Sodium pentothal," said the "doctor", throwing the syringe into a waste-paper basket. "Old-fashioned, as truth drugs go, but it's all I've got with me at the moment."

"Will it do the trick, Stanley?" asked the man standing behind Steve.

"Should do," answered Stanley, taking a tissue out of his jacket pocket and blowing his nose. "Think I'm getting a cold."

"Well, take it and your rubbish with you when you go," said the second man. "You can't just dump used syringes like that."

Steve knew something had gone wrong; he should have heard from Dachron and, right then, he'd have given anything to hear the man's gruff voice echoing round his head. Instead he was listening to the conversation, but not taking any of it in because he was feeling very strange.

Slowly but surely Steve was losing control: he couldn't

feel his hands or feet but he could feel his heart thundering away in his chest and he'd broken out in a cold sweat. Somewhere, in some distant part of his consciousness, he could hear a voice calling him; apart from the fact that he'd forgotten who it was, the voice was quite comforting. It was only when his muscles started to spasm and everything went black that he thought he was going to die. Which was exactly what the three men in the room thought as well.

"What's wrong with him, Stanley? He's not supposed to do that!"

"Idiot's overdosed the kid!"

"I did not, Dave!" said Stanley, rushing over to Steve and attempting to take his pulse. "Terry, you and Dave help me . . . get him on the floor and give me a biro or something!"

"Biro?"

"To put in his mouth, stop him swallowing his tongue."

By the time they'd got Steve's thrashing body on to the floor the spasms had subsided and he just lay there, his eyes rolled up so that only the whites were showing. His jaws gripped the plastic barrel of the ball-point pen like a vice.

"His pulse is all over the place!" said Stanley.

The man called Dave got up off the floor, went over to the phone on the wall and dialled a number. "Denner?" he said. "We've got a problem, big time – so *what* if you've seen the same milk float go past twice in five minutes – the kid's had some kind of fit and I think we should get him outta here, doublequick . . ."

"Damn!"

Tony looked up and saw Harker turn to the man monitoring the cameras and mics. "What?" he asked.

"Just heard someone talking about the milk float – I think they've sussed they're being watched, sir!"

"Put that bloody driver on a charge!" said Harker as he turned back to the console in front of him. "All units! This is Badger I – no more waiting, we have a go situation, I repeat, a go situation. They probably know we're here and we've got to get Tellkind out before *anything* can happen to him. Hit them, hit them hard, but remember that Tellkind's life is *far* too valuable to be put in danger!"

Where seconds before the TVs had shown empty streets surrounding the FPC building, Tony now saw two ground assault teams making for the front and rear entrances. That much he'd sort of expected, but the team abseiling down from the roof was something else.

"Will you look at that!" he whispered, scenes of hostage rescues from assorted SAS movies coming to mind. As he watched he saw the team at the front suddenly duck to either side of the front door as a small explosion went off. A second later the sound reached them in the Transit, a dull thud, followed by a second one. Tony moved to see the screens obscured by the man monitoring them; the rear entrance had been blown open as well.

"All units – switch to mini-cams," said Harker, and one by one the screens changed from clean, unwavering pictures to static-filled images that jumped all over the place as the men wearing the tiny cameras went into action.

Badger 2, the ground assault team led by Captain "Duke" Lord, ran through the shattered glass door and into the main foyer of the FPC building. The small charge of plastic had not only blown out the doors, but also cracked most of the windows as well, and when the sonic grenade went off two of them fell out into the street.

The sonic grenade basically blew out the eardrums of anyone in the vicinity and completely disoriented them. Badger 2, like the rest of the teams, all wore protective gear and were unaffected by the blast; they made straight for the stairs, leaving the ground floor to Badger 3 while Badger 4 handled the roof and second floor.

Captain Lord kicked open the doors at the top of the stairs and his No. 2 rolled another sonic grenade into the corridor; the moment it had exploded the onslaught continued. Armed men spilled out into the smoke-filled corridor, smashing open every door they came to and working their way around the whole floor with incredible speed.

A terrifyingly short fire fight broke out at one point when two men with blood streaming out of their ears tried unsuccessfully to hold a corner. Otherwise, from the sound of small-arms fire, the main resistance seemed to be coming from the floor above.

Captain Lord was making sure the two injured men were secured, if not comfortable, when he heard one of his men shouting for him.

"Civilian down, sir!" he yelled, waving from a room a few metres away.

"The target?" Lord shouted back as he ran.

"No, sir!"

Lord went into the room and saw the body of a young man, a teenager, on the floor. He was wearing a black jersey and jeans. "Wounded?" he said.

"Not by us, sir," said the soldier. "Think he's in some sort of coma, sir."

"Badger 2 Leader to Badger I – come in, Badger I," Lord spoke into his hands-free mic. "Medics needed, ASAP – ground and first secure, send them in!"

"That's Steve!" said Tony, pointing at the screen showing the body on the floor. "Is he dead?"

His question went ignored; Harker was yelling at someone to get him an Air Ambulance PDQ, whatever that meant, and the man monitoring the screens was relaying messages between the three assault teams.

"Roof! Someone making for the fire exit – armed, but wounded. First, watch the stairwell – could be some action," he turned to Harker. "ETA on the Air Ambulance, sir?"

"Two minutes."

"Badger I to Badger 2 Leader – Air Ambulance here in two, medics should be with you . . . get him ready to bring down."

There was nothing Tony could do but sit, watch and worry. The tension in the van was making the air sing; the sharp smell of sweat pricked his nose and his backside was going numb, but who was complaining? This was the most amazing experience of his life.

A burst of activity on one of the screens drew his eye and he saw a door smash open to reveal a man holding a gun to the head of a bespectacled academic-looking type.

"Badger 4 have found Tellkind, sir."

Harker looked round and took in the scene on the TV. "Tell them to stand back," he said, getting up out of his seat. "I'll go in and negotiate."

Outside the van Tony heard a roaring sound and knew it must be the helicopter. He glanced at the bank of TVs and saw two men carrying a stretcher, with another man running beside it holding a plasma bag up in the air. Its tube ran down into Steve's arm.

"Mr Harker?" he said, as the man walked past him to the rear doors.

"What?" he replied, staring at Tony as if he'd seen him for the first time.

"Can I go with Steve to the hospital, please?"

"Steve?"

"The boy they found, the one you got the helicopter for?" Tony jerked his thumb in the direction of the noise.

"He'll be under guard, sir," said the man at the screens.

"All right," Harker nodded at Tony, "come with me . . ."

24

Day 4 – Wednesday, 4th April 2007. 7.07 a.m.

The helicopter ride had been yet another amazing experience. The noise was absolutely incredible, a stuttering roar from the twin engines that made conversation impossible if you weren't wearing a soundproofed radio headset. Which he wasn't, and not that anyone would've talked to him anyway, thought Tony. The Air Ambulance's doctor and paramedic were frantically trying to work out what was wrong with Steve, while the pilot kept up an almost constant stream of babble with air traffic control.

Sitting with the medic Harker had told to go along, Tony spent the two short minutes it took to get to the Royal London taking in the view as the helicopter sped some sixty metres above London, on its way to the hospital's heliport. Before it had even touched down a team of doctors and nurses was running towards them with a trolley and seconds later Steve was being pushed at high speed into the hospital.

Tony ran after them, along with the medic. The man, he noticed, had a small sub-machine-gun slung over his back; what the *heck* were they guarding against? That worry was forgotten the moment he pushed past the swing doors and saw that Steve's trolley had stopped and everyone had gathered round it.

"He's fading!" Tony heard someone yell, and a doctor turned to the armed man next to him.

"Bring me up to speed," she said, beckoning him over.

"Discovered lying on the floor, irregular heartbeat, no obvious wounds," said the man breathlessly. "Noticed an injection mark on his left arm and found a used disposable syringe in a waste bin."

"Got it?"

"Right here," said the medic, taking a plastic bag out of one of his breast pockets and holding it out.

"Sister, take that up to the path. lab," the doctor said to one of the nurses, "and tell them I want to know what was in it *yesterday*. Now let's get to work on this boy!"

And off the trolley went, through some more doors and hard left into a waiting lift. Tony hung back, not knowing what he should do and not wanting to get in the way.

"Which floor?" asked the medic as the door closed.

"Second, neuro/tox," said the doctor.

"We'll take the stairs," said the medic. "There's no need for us to rush."

"Will he be all right?" asked Tony.

"I don't know . . . I'm sorry, what's your name?"

"Tony."

"Like I said, Tony, I've no idea if he'll be OK or not," said the medic as they started for the second floor. "But these guys are good; they'll do their best."

"What's neuro/tox?" asked Tony.

"Neurological and toxicological – nervous system and poisons."

"God, I hope he's not going to die!" Tony's shoulders

slumped and he suddenly felt completely drained. Something to do with not having eaten or slept for ages.

"He a relative or something?"

"No," said Tony, "just a friend."

"What was he doing in there?"

"Your guess is as good as mine." Tony stopped and looked at the man. "Are you pumping me for information?"

"What makes you think that?" The armed medic looked vaguely embarrassed at having been caught out.

"You're one of Mr Harker's men" – Tony squinted at the stencilled name patch on the man's body armour – "Sergeant Caddick."

By the time they got to where Steve had been taken it looked like he'd been hitched up to every available machine in the hospital. Wires and tubes trailed from his arms and head, everyone in the room seemed to be talking at once and at the centre of the storm he saw the dark-haired doctor.

"Has the path. test come back yet?" she said to no one in particular.

"No!"

"Well, someone go and make it happen!" shouted the doctor, peering at the read-out on a machine up by Steve's head.

Some lady! thought Tony, standing outside the room with the Sergeant, aware of what a bizarre sight the two of them must make in the midst of all this medical turmoil.

"There's something very strange here," said the doctor.

"Has this monitor been malfunctioning recently?"

"Don't think so. Why?" asked a prematurely balding young man.

"I'm getting two distinct alpha waves from the EEG," the doctor frowned, "both weak, but nonetheless two of them – look."

"From one person? That's just not possible!"

"True, Sam," nodded the doctor, "but unless this machine's suddenly gone on the friz, *that's* what it's picking up . . ."

Tony, whose mind had gone on to auto-pilot, snapped back. "What did she say?"

"The EEG's not working; it's showing two alpha waves," said the Sergeant, looking at him. "Are you OK? You've gone very pale."

"I'm fine," said Tony, but he was thinking, *two* alpha waves? What was it Steve had said to him last night when he'd gone all weird? He'd claimed to be another person, from the future, sharing his mind – and it looked like whoever had told him that wasn't lying – a double alpha wave could *only* mean two personalities in the one brain!

"Sodium pentothal!" shouted a voice from behind him, and a nurse pushed past into the room. "The lab says . . ."

"I heard . . . thiopentone sodium, a nasty old barbiturate. Which, if he's reacting like this, means his liver's having a *very* hard time." The doctor snapped her fingers. "Get the haemodialyser and someone find me a vein. We've got to try and clean him out!"

"Too late . . ." yelled the balding man, lunging at Steve's

chest and beginning to thump it. "His heart's stopped! We're losing him!"

Tony realized that the insistent beeping of Steve's heart monitor had changed to a continuous tone.

"Jump leads – and give me full power!" the doctor shouted, reaching out for the defibrillator pads. "Everyone stand back!"

A cold shiver ran down Tony's spine. As the doctor pumped electric shocks through Steve's jolting body – one . . . *pause* . . . two . . . *pause* . . . three – he had the truly horrible feeling that he was watching someone he knew die, right in front of him . . .

25

Day 6 – Friday, 6th April 2007. 2.15 p.m.

"Can I see him?" asked Tony. He felt better for having slept, but his nerves were still shot and he'd started chewing his nails again.

"You can go up now," said Harker.

Tony climbed the stairs and stopped outside the room, nervous at the thought of seeing Steve. He didn't know how he'd react; taking a deep breath he opened the door and walked in.

Steve, lying in the bed, looked like he was asleep. "You OK?" asked Tony, closing the door behind him.

"Feel like a horse kicked me," said Steve, turning to look at him. "What happened?"

Tony sat on the chair by Steve's desk and looked round at his bedroom before he answered. "You nearly died," he said.

That much at least was true. It had taken the medical team at the Royal London a full fifteen minutes to revive Steve after his heart had given out, fifteen minutes in which Tony had thought he might go into cardiac arrest as well. Only when he was sure that Steve was OK did he allow Sgt Caddick to take him away.

The weirdest thing was that when the doctor had

checked the "faulty" monitor, after Steve's heart had eventually started beating again, it had shown no sign of a double alpha wave. Only Tony realized this meant that Steve's companion – the person who'd said he was from the future – had gone.

A van had been waiting for them when they came out of the rear entrance to the hospital and he and Sgt Caddick had been whisked off to some nondescript office building in Acton. There he'd been fed, watered and given a camp bed to crash out on. Some time around five in the afternoon Mr Harker had woken him up and told him it was time for a debrief.

"Is Steve still all right?" asked Tony, sitting down opposite Harker.

"He's fine."

"What's going to happen to him?"

"Much of that depends on you, Tony," said Harker, leaning back in his chair and massaging his temples; he looked as beat as Tony felt.

"Me . . . how?"

Harker ignored the question and pushed a sheet of paper and a biro across the desk. "Sign that," he said.

"What is it?" The paper was upside down and Tony couldn't read what it said.

"The Official Secrets Act," said Harker tiredly. "Abide by it and you could well assure your future."

"But . . ."

"Stop arseing around and sign the damn thing!" said Harker, glowering at Tony. "I haven't got all day . . ."

Tony swivelled the piece of paper round and thought

about reading what it said, but he caught the look in Harker's eye and simply scribbled his name on the dotted line instead. "Whatever," he said, shoving it back across the desk.

Harker picked it up, folded it in half and put in the drawer in front of him without even looking at the signature. "That out of the way, let's get down to business," he said.

"What now?" enquired Tony.

"There are a few loose ends," said Harker, "and we need your help to tie them up."

"What can I do?"

"As far as we can tell, the young man, Steven Anthony, has no idea how he got into the FPC building," said Harker. "Under deep hypnosis he babbled some nonsense about someone called Dachron Amok taking over his brain. Was he on drugs? Did you see him taking any pills?"

Tony shook his head; Dachron Amok was the name Steve had used when he'd taken him back out to Docklands, ostensibly to find his trashed bike. Instead of saying anything Tony thought it better to keep that piece of information to himself; revealing it wouldn't help anyone.

"The fact is, no matter *how* he got in there," Harker continued, "it's down to the two of you that we found Simon Tellkind and broke the Future Power thing right open."

"So who is Simon Tellkind, and what's his connection with that bunch of crooks?" said Tony. "Or doesn't even signing my life away allow you to tell me?"

"Simon Tellkind is a scientist," said Harker. "He has

invented a new form of energy conversion, so efficient and pollution-free it's more of a miracle than an invention."

"And Future Power wanted to steal it?"

"He was working for Future Power," said Harker.

"So what was the big deal?"

"As you so cleverly proved the other night – doing things even our boys had failed to do, I should add" – Harker steepled his fingers and tapped his thumbs together – "Future Power is not at all what it seemed; as you now know, they're ultimately owned by an Eastern European energy cartel with the business manners of a pack of jackals."

"And nobody knew that?" asked Tony, frowning.

"We had our suspicions, but we didn't want to do anything until we were sure Tellkind had been successful," said Harker. "We had someone on the inside who was supposed to tip us off, but then everything went haywire and Tellkind disappeared."

"What were they going to do . . . Future Power, I mean?"

"Once they'd got the information off Tellkind?" Harker picked up a pencil and began doodling on the pad in front of him. "Hold the world to ransom, basically."

"What?" Tony sat back in surprise. "How?"

"Think about it, Tony . . . You own the rights to what will undoubtedly be the motive power for the twenty-first century, and beyond, and you're already in the extortion business," Harker smiled wanly. "What would *you* do?"

"Make people pay through the nose for it?"

"Damn right."

"And now you've got it?" asked Tony.

"Damn right again." This time Harker grinned like a monkey. "But we're the good guys."

"And me, how do I fit into all this? Didn't you say something about assuring my future . . . ?"

"I nearly *died*?" said Steve, slowly sitting up. "How?"

Tony knew he was going to hate himself for doing this, but he also knew he had no choice. Harker had him painted into a corner: he was on the payroll now. "They think you went into some sort of coma . . . after falling off your bike," he said, looking out of the bedroom window.

"*Fell off*?" said Steve angrily. "I was forced off the road by that car, the one that chased us!"

"Whatever, Steve," Tony glanced at him. "They say it was brought on by concussion – they had to kick-start your heart, you know . . . that's why you feel like you've been booted about."

"Coma . . ." muttered Steve, shaking his head and staring off into the middle distance as his fingers picked at the duvet cover. His mind whirled in confusion as half-remembered images flashed in and out of view – men with guns, people shouting at him, someone with a syringe giving him an injection. He pulled up his sleeve, looked at his arm and saw a small yellowy-grey bruise. "This is too weird . . ."

"What is?" Tony felt very uncomfortable; he wanted to go, but thought he should stay a little longer.

"Everything," said Steve. In his head there was a curious empty sensation, almost like being in a room you knew very well, though one from which you were also sure something important was missing. And then he remembered. No Dachron.

"Are you OK?" asked Tony. "You look kinda pale all of a sudden."

"What day is it?" said Steve.

"Friday . . . afternoon, about 2.30."

"What happened to Thursday?"

"You slept through it, guy." Tony got up. "Look, I've got to make a move. I just wanted to make sure you were all right, and tell you they found your bike and it's been fixed, got a new front wheel."

"Terrific."

"Yeah." Tony moved towards the door. "The doctors say you're, like, fully back up to speed and they – you know, the police – got hold of your au pair and she's back now, so there's someone here and everything's back to normal . . ."

"See you, then." Steve half waved, wondering why Tony was babbling. Wondering why nothing seemed to make any sense.

"Yeah, later," said Tony.

"But what happened to Simon Tellkind?" said Steve as Tony was starting to close the door.

Tony caught his breath. "Simon who?" he queried, hoping he sounded genuine. Was Steve playing games with him?

Steve shook his head. "Nothing," he said, suddenly remembering that he'd told Tony it was his father who was in trouble. "Forget it."

26

Day 6 – Friday, 6th April 2007. 2.43 p.m.

"Did he buy it?" asked Harker when Tony came out of the house.

"I think so. He's very confused, though," said Tony.

"No surprise there, then."

"He mentioned Tellkind," said Tony, watching Harker to see how he'd respond to that piece of information.

"Not a problem," he replied, walking towards a car parked down the street. "Tellkind, to all intents and purposes, doesn't exist any more."

"Oh?"

"He's alive and well," explained Harker, opening the rear passenger door and indicating that Tony should get in, "but we've taken him out of circulation until the dust's settled. He's ours now."

"So it's all over?" said Tony. As he slid across the seat he saw a tall, good-looking girl walking towards them.

"It will be soon," replied Harker, slamming the door, "when all the papers are lodged with the Patent Office on Monday morning. All tied up and neatly sorted."

"Like it never happened."

"You saw the news last night," said Harker.

"Some story," nodded Tony. As the car moved off he saw the girl stop in front of the gate to Steve's front garden.

"I liked it." Harker reached into his breast pocket, took out an envelope and gave it to Tony. "This is for you. Think of it as back pay . . . Professor Horowitz will let you know what happens next."

Outside in the street car doors slammed and an engine turned over. Downstairs Steve heard the buzzer go. He'd let Nadja get it, he thought. He didn't feel like rushing to answer the front door. He lay in bed for a moment, wondering what to do, and then he realized he felt very hungry.

"Wonder if there's anything to eat," he said to himself, gingerly getting out of bed. He felt a little light-headed, but that soon passed; on the back of a chair by his desk he could see all his clothes. "Cleaned," he said, starting to get dressed.

There was a newspaper on his chest of drawers and Steve unfolded it and read the front page as he buttoned up his shirt. "DRUGS RING BROKEN!" screamed the bold headline; underneath it was a grainy colour picture of the Future Power building, most of its front windows blown out.

He checked the dateline: Thursday 5th April, the late edition of the *Evening Standard*. He sat down on his swivel chair and read the day-old story. An undercover police operation, it said, had closed down a major international drugs dealing enterprise – linked, so the reporter believed, directly to the Russian Mafia. The story went on to give a breathless account of what had happened in the dawn raid, detailing what it called "the SAS-like" attack on the building and the resulting death and injury toll – one man killed, five still in hospital with gunshot wounds and under heavy guard, no police casualties.

Not a mention of him or Simon Tellkind.

Had *any* of it happened, or had the whole insane, crazed few days been a complete figment of his imagination? He knew Dachron had been there, but then every mad person was absolutely sure that the voices in their head were real – why should he be any different?

Steve put the paper down. His stomach was complaining about the lack of food and he really fancied a cup of tea – maybe he could persuade Nadja to make him one of her awesome cheese and ham omelettes. He was halfway downstairs when he saw his bike propped up in the hall – they'd brought it back, with a new front wheel, as promised!

He walked down the rest of the stairs and went over to it, swung his leg over the saddle and gripped the handlebars. Slowly he tried to pull out the right-hand one and twist it, and . . . nothing. It wouldn't budge. He got off and looked closely at the bike.

"All brand new . . ." he whispered. "The whole bloody lot!"

He stood up. That was it. He had no proof whatsoever that anything had *ever* happened. No proof that a man from the future had risked his life to come back to save the world from ultimate disaster – and no idea whether he'd succeeded or not. He didn't believe a word of Tony's story about a coma – he knew Dachron had taken over again when he'd gone to sleep – knew *he'd* woken up in the Future Power building with no notion how he'd got there.

Steve had no idea why he hadn't heard from Dachron, but the fact was he wasn't there any more. And the other, even stranger fact was – he missed him. Life with another person inside his head had been undeniably strange, but life without him was odd too, lonely somehow. No doubt he'd get used to it. But one thing Steve was sure of, he'd *never* forget . . .

"Steve?" said a voice from down the hall.

He looked up. "Ellie!" he grinned, all thoughts of loneliness evaporating. "Boy, is it good to see you!"

27

Spenzer Timor had returned to Central Data Control, fifty floors up in a Johannesburg office tower, mere hours after the "soul pilot", Dachron Amok, had been sent on an epic journey. Spenzer's job now was to immerse himself in the information streams to see whether Project Take-Over had worked. He'd been in constant virt contact with the team in Pretoria, every one of them on tenterhooks as they waited for some kind of confirmation.

Cloistered in his room he'd sat, literally on the edge of his seat, and waited for the signs – positive or negative – to register. Almost immediately senior technicians at a secret test lab had come on-line to tell him that even the most delicate equipment they, or their colleagues at Dallas and Arecibo, had was failing to pick up any subatomic exhaust! An extraordinary piece of news in itself, but there was soon to be more.

Slowly but surely, it became clear that across the globe things were getting back to normal – no more extreme geographical and weather anomalies, and a gradual return to the status quo. Somehow, 600 years in the distant past, Dachron Amok had seemingly done the impossible and allowed history to be rewritten. As he worked, Spenzer wondered about how he'd done it, what it must have been like to go back and live another life. What had happened to him? Had it been dangerous? Had the override lasted longer than the predicted seven days? Questions that would never be answered, so hardly worth asking, but they were there in Spenzer's head nonetheless.

The whole concept of time travel was outrageous, beyond reason, but according to all the data it had actually happened – a man he'd once known (however fleetingly) had made an inconceivable journey and obviously survived. If not to tell the tale, then to leave absolute evidence of his having been there. Against all odds, Project Take-Over had worked!

By Day 4 Project Take-Over was deemed a total and complete success – there was, according to all available facts, figures and statistics, absolutely no sign of the dreaded Scattering Effect. But, relieved and happy as he was – and looking forward to a major celebration with the rest of the team – Spenzer was left with one sad image.

Somewhere in a building in downtown Pretoria, what was left of a man who had once been Dachron Amok lay strapped to a chair. Although Spenzer was more than overjoyed that the world he lived in was no longer in danger of self-destructing, he felt guilty about being responsible for the death of the man in the Ejector Seat.

Albeit there was still enough basic brain activity to keep the man's body functioning, it was very much at a vegetable level; he was dead, from a human point of view, even if no one had actually taken the decision to switch him off permanently. Yet. And Spenzer felt responsible because he was the person who had chosen Line Sgt Amok, recommended him, put his name forward as the best person – the *only* person – for the job.

He felt like an executioner.

Only a handful of people in the entire world would ever know what had happened – members of the most exclusive club, and one destined to remain a total secret – but Spenzer would know what he'd done, and his pride would always be tempered with a sense of melancholy. Maybe, like Stave Barron had said, the world would be a better place without soldiers . . . but there would have been no world in the future without Dachron Amok.

Dachron's work was now done and life, thanks to him and the rest of the team, would go on. Spenzer stopped staring out of the window of his fiftieth-floor office and tried to concentrate on a new Arctic dataset when the red light warning him of an incoming holocast came on and the virt image of Vena Cardoza, head of the Science Agency out in Maraisburg, snapped into view. She looked confused and excited at the same time, most unlike the cool, calm scientist he thought he knew.

"Spenzer," she said, "I think you should come out here . . . now."

"Maraisburg?" said Spenzer. "Why – what's the matter, Vena?"

"Not Maraisburg – the Take-Over building," said Vena. "And I'll explain when you get here."

The holocast abruptly finished and Spenzer was left wondering what on earth was going on – why was Vena acting so oddly? As far as he knew there was just a skeleton staff of technicians and a medic or two left out in Pretoria monitoring Dachron's life-support systems – why was Vena still there? Only one way to find out.

"Transport!" Spenzer yelled at the comms screen nearest him. "Get me a shuttle, please . . . Priority 1."

"When did it happen?" asked Spenzer, hardly able to take in what he was seeing.

"Fifteen minutes before I called you, and everyone else," replied Vena.

"What were you doing here?"

"Josh and I decided to stay . . . we couldn't just go and leave him here on his own, being looked after by the techs" – she nodded at the window that gave into the TRiP room – "not after what he did. And now, with what's just happened, I'm really glad."

Spenzer was in the same room, staring through the same plate-glass window that he'd last been in with Stave Barron. The day they'd sent Dachron Amok away.

"How did it happen?" he asked.

"Josh has no idea," said Vena. "He says the only possibility is that *somehow* someone must've replicated at least two of the system's main components."

"Which ones?"

"He thinks it has to be a combination of a major dose of a hypnotic drug, followed by the application of a series of high-voltage shocks," explained Vena. "Though quite why anyone'd do that is totally beyond me."

"But *how* did he zero back home?"

"All Josh said was something like 'a memory has memory'," said Vena, shrugging. "Make of that what you will . . . but I'll tell you something – are we going to have some party now!"

"Can we go in?" Spenzer pointed through the glass.

"Sure."

Spenzer walked over to the door and went into the room the other side of the glass. "Hi, Dachron," he said, a broad smile on his face. "How d'you feel?"

Dachron was still in the chair, impatiently waiting for all the wires to be detached. "Like I've been kicked by a horse," he said.